I0725554

There are so many to thank and yet trying to list them is difficult.
Keri, Suzi, Sassie, Tee, Michelle, Susan... All part of my tribe!
Makers & Fakers! You guys seriously rock! Thank you for your awesome
support whether it's a rocky patch or perfection.
To Pamela & Willsin for editing and covers that simply rock my world.
To my husband Mark and Miss C...
To my awesome readers who've invested in this series. Thank you.

Imogene Nix
Kingaroy
2021

FINIS: THE WAR TO END ALL WARS

21st Testing Protocol

Imogene Nix

Love Books Publishing

Copyright © 2021 by Imogene Nix®

All rights reserved.

No part of this book may be reproduced in any form or by any electronic or mechanical means, including information storage and retrieval systems, without written permission from the author, except for the use of brief quotations in a book review.

This book is a work of fiction. Character, places and events are from the author's imagination and should not be confused with fact. Any resemblance to persons, living or dead, events or places is purely coincidental.

Print ISBN 978-1-922369-33-8

CHAPTER 1

Senna Reed poked at the meal on her plate. "Slop, more like," she muttered. It was an unappetizing mess, and not for the first time, she considered how her life had come full circle. Back on a base again, eating military grub, wasn't quite what she'd envisioned when she'd returned to civilian life.

The meat was dewy at best, or better described as downright wet. The vegetables erred on the side of overcooked, and she wasn't the only one feeling the pain of the bad food standards. With a sigh, she shunted the plate away then rose. If there was nothing edible, she refused to waste any more of her time.

"There isn't even an herb or condiment to be seen," she said.

Out the doorway, she caught sight of the orange light in the sky and wondered, as she always seemed to these days, what the cause was. Since the lockdown of the base, the excursions to the city were limited to targeted attacks, the odd mission to extract personnel, or guard duty for traveling officials.

Cupping her hand over her brow, she ignored the trickle of sweat that slid down her back. Summer was on its way with a vengeance, and things were only likely to get worse once the real heat settled in.

"They hit the last of the hospitals. Saint Jory's security contacted us at 2000 hours to advise they were surrounded."

She whirled at the voice then sighed heavily. "Mann. Next time, some warning would be useful. Civilian losses?"

Franklin Mann. She'd first met him years ago, when he'd been a guard for Dr. Michael Villede. Not that he needed one now, given both he and his wife were cyber-enhanced with super-strength. Senna snorted but stilled the sound when Mann pinned her with his dark brown gaze.

Mann was a long-time pain in the ass, all brawn and not so much brain. He tended to lumber around, beefcake-like, but she had to give him credit for his fighting style. Most people took him cheap, thinking he'd be too heavy to move quickly, but there was an unusual grace to him when it came to hand-to-hand combat.

"My contacts say minimal. Mostly the site was cleared after we sent the first alert. Only the most necessary cases were still in situ. Still, the loss of medical personnel won't help the greater community."

Senna frowned at his assessment. She rarely had the opportunity to talk to the man, having drawn her conclusions remotely. Yet, he'd summed up everything she'd wanted to know with brevity. It made her wonder if she'd sold him short.

"Your sources?" she asked.

He shrugged and glanced away. "I know some people who know other people."

A moment passed, then another. The need to twitch rising which angered her. Senna realized he'd say nothing more unless directly asked, and it irked. "Okay, thanks."

She took off, heading across the parade grounds in the direction of the offices, aware her particular skillset might be required by Daniella and Jonah.

So much had changed in such a short while, she mused. Daniella had become the head of the resistance, and Jonah had assumed the position of Base Leader.

Her own team of arson investigators had been scattered after the first major attack by the children. "If someone had mentioned even a modicum of what happened in the last few months, I would have laughed at them."

From the corner of her eye, she spied movement and turned, then breathed freely once more when she realized it was David and Erin. Their weariness was clear in the droop of their shoulders and married with the soot on their faces.

"Tough night?" Senna asked.

Erin's lips firmed, white lines edging the pink flesh. "An attack on Saint Jory's. About sixty lost, mainly ICU staff and patients."

Senna growled. Always just too late, but that was what she'd trained for, wasn't it? Right now there was no satisfaction in knowing she'd be able to tell them when and how. "Dammit. What do you need from me?"

David shook his head. "We may need your skills with explosives, finding what they hit the building with, but until then, we just need to get clean, some food—"

"Avoid the mess hall then."

David glowered while Erin sputtered. "This is hard enough on good food. When it's bad, it's unbearable. What was it today?"

"Overcooked and really wet meat. They tried to pass it off as stew."

"Urgh." David shuddered. "Maybe we'll just pop on over to the infirmary then. I'm sure Michael and Clarissa will have something better on offer."

"So I hear. Maybe they could teach those who are on cook duty a few things?" Senna snarled.

"I'll mention it to Daniella. Now, if you'll excuse us, I'm not so sure I don't stink of some charred things I don't want to consider." David tugged on his wife's hand, and Erin waved goodbye as they trudged off.

Once gaining the interior of the office space, Senna was stopped by a small woman rocking a baby at the front desk. If she didn't know better, she'd call this unattached woman almost maternal. However, today, she could also add the tag of 'gatekeeper'.

"Senna, what can you do for us today?"

Senna blinked at the strange query. Maylin was the resident data and technological wizard of the base. Had she decided to adopt one of the children they'd found in the laboratory just two months ago?

"I didn't realize you were chosen, Maylin! Congratulations on your new child!"

The woman eyed her with an intense glare. "I wasn't. I'm simply sitting until his mother can return." She grimaced. "I have no intention of breeding or fostering." The baby waved its arms and gurgled before a large, smelly emanation came from the region of its bottom.

Taking a step back, Senna waved her hands, hoping to ward off the stench. Maylin looked downright horrified and stared at the being in her arms.

"I've come to see the senator or Jonah if either are available?"

"Daniella is meeting with members of the resistance, but Jonah will be here in a couple of minutes. I just hope the mother turns up quickly and takes this bundle of joy home. *Soon.*"

Maylin's scrunched face told Senna everything she wanted to know. "Okay, thanks." She moved away from the desk, and around the corner, perching on the hard, plastic chair while waiting for Jonah to arrive.

*F*ranklin watched as Senna, a tall, dark-haired woman, strode purposefully away. He wondered if she were dismissive of his talents. Hell, he was damned good in the field, but not a strategist, and he was aware she was well-regarded as an investigator with the arson team. It wasn't so much that she was so totally beyond him in terms of her rank—though even back when they were both in the services, she held a higher position—it was more the air about her.

On an indrawn breath, he turned and headed away from the mess hall. According to Senna, there wasn't really anything in there worth eating, and he had a standing invitation with Michael and Clarissa.

At the door to the infirmary he cast a glance down the corridor. It was quiet. A whole heap more than he would ordinarily expect.

His footsteps echoed on the tiles, the scent of cleanser and lemon filling his nostrils.

He'd missed the camaraderie from the days when he'd been guarding Michael. Back then Michael had been an up-and-coming officer with a bright future, while Franklin had been a private first class. He'd moved on of course. His field promotion to army specialist during the war wasn't something he talked about a lot. It come at great personal cost, when his platoon commander realized he was handy with a rifle and long-range sniping.

His mind shied away from the memory of what he'd done and how many times he'd dealt with a difficult situation for those in senior ranks. What it had achieved for his platoon was to give them a fighting chance more than once in the middle of a skirmish.

He scowled as the familiar need to work off tension suddenly filled his body like a tide washing over him.

The urgency to stop, turn around, and run—far and hard enough to forget—became a clawing beast, tearing at his guts, and he had to lean against the wall and breathe, sucking in great lungfuls of air until the sensation passed.

Dots popped before his eyes, gray and black, until he was once again able control his body.

"Franklin?" The voice at the end of the corridor captured his attention, and he managed to gather his senses enough to paste on a smile.

"Clarissa. God, I hope you've got something edible cooking."

She hurried forward, her hands reaching for his and drawing his close. If he hadn't known better, he would have thought her just a normal, if average, woman. Well, if you discounted the weird light emanating from her eyes.

"Are you sick? Do you need to see Michael?"

Franklin sighed. "I'm okay. Just thought of something and it sort of knocked me flat. Don't worry though. I'm good."

He gazed into her eyes, willing her forcefully to understand and let go of her concerns. It must have worked as the tension in her grasp fizzled away. "If you say so. And yes, I have food cooking. Some basic stew, but it will be filling."

Clarissa urged him forward beyond the patient area and into the private living zone she'd claimed together with her husband, Michael, and the child they'd adopted.

"How's the baby?"

"Oh, fine. Growing. Like quickly. Erin and David are joining us once they've had a chance to clean up. They've been out all night dealing with the explosion at Saint Jory's. Daniella and Jonah were coming, but she's tied up with the resistance, and I'm not sure what Jonah is doing. Now sit down at the table. It won't be long."

Scents of stewing meat and vegetables filled the air, and his stomach gurgled its approval of what would soon be forthcoming. "Want me to do something?"

Clarissa disappeared into the room beyond then came back, a small bundle in her arms, that was until she deposited it into his arms. "Feed the baby for me while I finish getting everything ready."

He cradled the child awkwardly until she shoved the small bottle into his hand.

"Like this." With a firm motion, Clarissa guided the nipple to the baby's mouth. It latched on, rapacious mouth moving in a quick rhythm as it sucked. The sound of gulps and the sight of bubbles his immediate reward. Then Clarissa left the room.

"Have you given her a name yet?"

Clarissa popped her head through the doorway. "They all had designations when they were found, but Michael and I needed some time to agree on a name. She deserved better than a weird designation, so we combed through some ancient texts, in the hopes we'd find something inspiring. And we did. I can't remember the name of the book, but there was a character called Eliza Doolittle who rose above her station and achieved something no one thought possible. That appealed so much, we decided to call her Eliza."

"Huh!" Franklin glanced down to the infant he was sure was

listening intently. "Hi, Eliza. I'm Uncle Franklin, and you've got a great family. We're all here for you."

The baby released the bottle on a sigh and burped loudly, as if in agreement.

"Doing a great job there, Uncle Frank!" Erin's words made him jump, and the baby screwed up her face as if to cry then relaxed as Erin slid a finger down her cheek. "How you doing, sweetie? Want to come to Auntie Erin?"

Franklin wasn't sure if he felt relieved or sad at the sudden loss of weight as Erin lifted the baby from his arms. Instead, he simply turned and gave a single nod to David who stood watching his wife settle the baby at her shoulder and smoothing circles over her tiny back.

"Here for dinner?" Clarissa ushered them to the table. "Won't be more than a moment or two."

⁂

Senna settled into the seat opposite Jonah. "I heard about the explosion and those who died. I'm so sorry. I wondered if I could be of assistance."

Jonah rubbed red, tired eyes. "That would be great, but to be honest, that's less important than getting to the person at the bottom of this mess."

"But do you know who the ringleader is? I thought it was hidden. A matter of state secrecy."

Jonah steepled his fingers. "We think we do, and yes, Daniella has put in place certain need-to-know protocols. If this information gets out, and when you take into account the situation with Phenja, I dread to think what will happen next. We have to track down Lilly Montaine, but it's like we're stumbling around in the dark. Topping off all of this, we have the first colony ship ready, with a projected lift-off date very soon. Then we've got the creches where they are creating and growing these children."

He stopped and slumped, elbows on his desk.

"We have so many competing priorities, and all the while, we're sitting ducks here on the base." Jonah grunted and shook his head. The pressure must have been building, as Jonah rubbed at the pounding between his eyes. "They've already breached our defenses more than once, Senna. We need to lock this down now, clear some of the issues so we can target our efforts."

Senna agreed with his assessment. It made no sense why they'd attacked Saint Jory's. By taking out one of the last remaining hospitals in the city, the populace had nowhere to turn in times of need. There had to be some reason.

"But why Saint Jory's, Jonah?"

He shook his head. "We haven't worked that out yet. But while it's an answer we really need, we don't have the time or resources to—"

"And that's where I disagree, respectfully. I'm sure there's something about it that will give us a hint. People don't remove structures like that without a good and valid reason."

"I understand your reasoning but—" Jonah spread his hands.

"No. My training as an arson investigator tells me there's something hinky about this. Give me some time—a day or two to see what I can learn. If this doesn't work..."

"I can't, Senna. I need you on tracking down Lilly Montaine." Jonah sounded defeated.

"Let one of the others—" she urged.

"No. I'm over-ruling you. Once we have her brought to heel—"

"The evidence will be gone. Come on, Jonah, twenty-four hours is all I'm asking for. Time to run the CCTV footage and on-site time. I can go alone. Twenty-four hours, and if I don't find any useful info, I'll drop it until after we find Montaine." Senna leaned forward, urgency in every word she spoke.

Jonah sighed and settled back into the squabs of the chair. "You drive a hard bargain. But not alone. Take Franklin with you for protection so you can concentrate fully on the task. But I can only spare one day."

"All right." She nodded, then allowed her brain to switch to the next matter. "Now, tell me about Montaine."

CHAPTER 2

Franklin couldn't say what it was that rankled about his sideways shift to support and guard Senna on her way to the site that had been Saint Jory's Hospital. For all that, he'd been instructed by Jonah to do so. *Suck it up, Franklin.*

He'd been a guard before, so he knew the routine, though looking after Michael had been simple enough during the war. The task may have begun on the battlefield, but soon thereafter they'd transferred to one of the field hospitals. All the top-flight medicos had guards, and they'd doubled up as orderlies. Franklin had quickly grown accustomed to the duality of that role.

This time was different, what with his target climbing over a bomb site, delving into nooks and crannies, more than aware that below both of them lay the remains of shattered bodies.

"Hey, Mann!"

His head jerked in Senna's direction, and he noted with dismay she was tugging at piles of rubble, working steadily, wearing a pair of glasses that seemed to drag off her face. "What are you doing?" he asked as he clambered toward her, and she glanced toward him.

She grunted, lifting what appeared to be a larger block of debris. "I'm checking for chemical residue that would give me a clue as to the makeup of the bomb. I can already see traces of something, but I need to get further down to access samples I can take away."

"Can't you just scrape it off?"

The look she shot at him was clear. If eyes could talk, hers would be calling him several kinds of fool right now. So, he waited; at some point Senna would explain what she needed.

"No. That could contaminate the evidence with metal from the blade or other things. I need a larger sample, one I can carry, to take back and check through in a clean lab. If I can get a large enough sample, I won't need the specialist equipment in the investigative lab at the firehouse."

"You won't need any special equipment?"

She kept rooting around. "No. I have a lot of my own equipment because it was a 'boys club'."

Franklin was still caught on the access to the lab. "What do you—"

"I was on restriction beforehand, and the labs are located in the middle of the city. Besides, even before that, I had to fight for lab time, and I doubt Jonah will let me go to the central fire office. I need to use what I have available, and that's why I need your help to get this bloody sample. So, do you think you can stop asking questions?"

He inched forward and watched as she carefully removed a block, then another until a gap appeared.

When Franklin reached forward, Senna stopped him. "No. See that black and silver marking? That's what I need." She pointed to a smallish block that sat some distance from the opening.

"And how do you—"

Senna blinked then smiled. "I'm going to climb down, while you hold a line for me and retrieve it."

He backed up, shaking his head, his feet sliding and crunching on the shards of broken building. "No. You're not going down into the hole. Jonah would have my head on a platter if anything happened to you."

"And it won't, because you'll be keeping me safe. The debris here is fairly solid, so dropping down is the only way I can get it. Franklin,

I only have today to get this sample. After that, he's going to pull me off investigating, and *this is important*. It could tell us something we don't already know."

He sighed, aware that Jonah had only allowed her one day to visit the site and scan the footage of the explosion. What if it gave them some clue or link as to how to beat the warrior children? To track down Montaine and defeat those who showed total disregard for life.

"Okay, but you're on a rope," he said firmly. "*And* if I say we have to get out of here, we do, without complaint. Yes?"

She opened her mouth to remonstrate, it was there in her narrowed gaze, but after long, fraught seconds she gave a nod. "Okay."

Franklin dropped his satchel and hunted for the rope he'd stashed. Senna took it and draped it around her waist. With a couple of firm movements she had it knotted so it wouldn't unravel easily and waited only for his "okay" before she climbed into the hole. She moved cautiously, slipped in feet first, then slid down over the edge she'd created.

When only her hands and head remained out, she gazed at him. "Ready?"

"Sure. Why not?" he muttered, and she smiled, then dropped out of view.

The rope became taut, and he moved one step then another forward, until he was standing over the hole. Glancing down, he noted the play of light from her hand-held light.

"Got it?" he asked.

He heard the grunts of her efforts. "Not yet. Just a moment more."

The rope swayed and he frowned, watched her tug at the rubble firmly embedded in the debris with a couple of grunts. He groaned and realized the sample she'd indicated wasn't releasing as easily as she'd hoped. Time was of the essence as the sun rose in the sky, and the jitters in his belly started. He trusted those jitters, aware they'd never before steered him wrong.

"We need to hurry," Jonah said.

"Just a moment," she called, and he ground out an oath.

"We don't have time, Senna." The awareness that they were no longer alone was reinforced by the visage of a single child watching from the far end of the ruins. "They're here."

"Damn!" she cursed. "Okay, I've got it. Get me out of here."

He tugged fast and hard, hand moving over hand while the rope seared the palms of his hands. Quickly, she pushed the rock free of the hole and hauled herself out.

"We need to get out of here," he murmured as she bent.

Senna retrieved her treasure, and together, they moved in the direction of the vehicle, their feet picking the way through the rubble of the hospital's remains.

The faster they moved, the more urgent the jitters became. The vehicle waited just at the edge, and he wanted to know how close the children were, but he couldn't risk losing time or his footing.

In the distance came the echo of pounding feet. At the car, he reached for the doors, shoved inside as she did. "Hang on," he yelled while he punched the ignition button. The engine fired and he floored the gas pedal.

The vehicle shot forward, and his glance in the mirror told him they'd just got away in time as a band of children reached the location of the vehicle's parking spot.

"That was a bit too close for my liking," whispered Senna, and he looked in her direction, where she slumped in the seat, the lump of masonry cradled in her hands and both eyes closed. It was the pallor of her skin that gave away her awareness of just how close they'd come.

"You got what you needed though, right?"

She cracked open one eyelid and watched him for a long, tense second. "Oh yes, Franklin. I did. The smell of it tells me lots already as do the striations of the break. If the chemical signature is what I think it is though, it will answer more than a few questions. Let's get back to the base so I can get started."

He barked a laugh. "I was ready to come back before you found that bit of rock."

"Perhaps. But I'm pretty sure this lump will give us an upper hand. I'll explain more later. Once I've had time to check the compounds used and know for sure."

With that, he accepted the dismissal from Senna. It rankled, but hell, he was just the glorified babysitter, so he shrugged and drove as quickly as he could back to the base.

CHAPTER 3

Senna slid open the satchel she'd stashed before leaving the arson squad headquarters and removed the psionic scalpel. The small earbuds that would protect her hearing were shoved into place. She'd already hung a sign on the door warning people not to enter. The last thing she needed was some stray portion getting into an eyeball of someone without the appropriate protection, or worse, a chemical reaction making someone sick.

The light she'd appropriated from the bedside wasn't quite what she was used to in a laboratory setting, but it would do well enough to illuminate her thrown together workspace. The small eye protectors she shoved against her face scratched at the sensitive skin, but she ignored that. Her whole focus now rested on the lump of smashed masonry. Last, she applied the mask.

"I look like some science experiment," she muttered then pushed the thought away.

Setting the switch of her implement to *on*, she gripped the handle with a firm grasp and started the process of slicing off enough to access the chemical markers. Thin, she thought as the scalpel slid through the mass. A tiny piece fell away and dropped onto the padding she'd wadded below. Turning off the scalpel, she popped it down on the workbench and picked up the tweezers.

Senna lifted the small piece she'd carved off, inspected it. "Hope it's enough," she murmured and slipped it into the tube which already held the chemical reagents. Breathing deeply, hoping to quell the sudden racing of her pulse, she watched and waited. A bubble started, then the chemicals turned from pink to blue, and she sighed. "Just as I thought."

She slid the test tube into the small, wooden holder, picked up her pen, and wrote down the findings, what chemicals she'd used, and the process. She had to be able to replicate it if required.

Then she hefted her communications device, snapped a picture of the process, the color change, and the notes she'd made.

"Triacetone triperoxide." The chemical was one she knew she'd seen before, in fact, several times over the last six months in increasing and concerning repetition, even though it was considered an ancient form of explosive.

Slumping in the seat, she simply stared at the lump and sighed. *Time to contact Jonah.* Pressing the screen of the communicator, she hailed him.

"I have news, Jonah."

"Senna?"

"Yeah. I've discovered what they're using to effect these attacks. They're using an ancient type of explosive called triacetone triperoxide. It relies on a weak oxygen-to-oxygen bond, and I've been seeing this over the last about six months... Slow initially but increasingly popular."

"And?"

"The rest of the investigators I know couldn't name a perpetrator. But then, neither could I, until now." Senna inhaled deeply. "Prior to the last year, this explosive was one we learned about during arson training history, but it wasn't more than a cursory glance. It makes sense now, because it's easy to obtain the ingredients, can be made at home, and detonators are pretty easy to come by for this particular compound. Jonah, they used to call this stuff the 'Mother of Satan'."

He blinked slowly on the screen then gave a slow nod. "Can we detect it before they ignite it?"

She shrugged. "There used to be ways from what I remember, but I'd need to dig up more information before we can set anything in motion. In the training we were just introduced to these compounds as something of interest. Everyone thought them archaic, and I would guess no one actually expected to come across them now. As for detecting trace elements, they're easier to detect after ignition. Beforehand is...well..." Senna spread her hands.

Without some way to detect it prior to detonation, they were in a precarious position.

"So, what does this mean? Senna, if this is an undetectable compound, we're unable to prepare for this eventuality."

She grimaced. "I know. I'll move as quickly as I can, but I can't use my usual resources. I'll need access to the ultranet to confirm and some time to research more."

"It can't be via a connected system." His face appeared tight, as if it were just one more dangerous situation to work through on little to no time or sleep.

"No, I won't use a connected system, Jonah. I'll talk to Maylin tomorrow if you can send the requisition through expedited channels. See if she can scare something up for me to use. Maybe use one of the older systems, because they have differing layers of encryption and access, and I doubt they'll be monitoring those systems. I know what I'm looking for, *if* it's out there, but who knows?"

He grunted. "Good work picking up on this."

"Thanks. I'm going to head over to the mess. Grab something to eat, then an early night. I don't think there's much more I can achieve tonight." To be honest, exhaustion washed over her. Perhaps some fresh air and food would clear the sluggishness that wanted to settle into her system.

"All right, I'll flick that requisition through. Just remember to update me with whatever you find. More knowledge will help us reinforce our borders."

She disconnected and sat still for a moment. Aware that she'd helped them to make an important finding. The only thing was, could she find them a way to overcome the mess?

On a sigh, she rose and began clearing away her impromptu laboratory. Old habits died hard, she thought as she shoved the masonry shaving and chunk of rock into the bottom of her lockbox and headed out.

⊰·❦·⊱

Franklin Mann looked at the pile of mush they'd served up in the mess. Glutinous and gray, it resembled something he'd rather not think about. It was food, and he'd been assured nutritious, but that didn't improve how it looked.

The fact was though, their food security was tenuous at best. The attacks on the convoys attempting to enter the base were becoming more vicious each time, and efforts being made at bringing in victuals through other avenues remained a band-aid solution.

At his shoulder, a woman hovered, and he raised his head, the fork hovering between the plate and his mouth.

"Mind if I join you?"

Senna.

The arson investigator had tweaked his interest, but he doubted a beef-cake kind of guy like him was of interest to her. He wasn't one to waste his efforts, so with a cautious smile, he indicated the seat was free, then returned his gaze to the food. He stabbed at a chunk but didn't raise it to his mouth.

"I hear the engineers think there are only a couple more weeks until the first of the colony ships depart."

The huskiness in her voice floated around him. Then he startled, glanced up. "How did you find that out?"

"I heard it from someone working with the grunts. Reckons they're going to lock down the base tighter than before to make sure there's no incursions by the kids."

His gaze narrowed on her spoon as it traveled between her luscious, pink lips. "And?"

She waited a moment. A long, pregnant moment.

He blinked. "And so..."

"I've got a problem, Franklin Mann, and you're the one I need assistance from."

Funny, he could swear the woman beside him was capable of just about anything without any assistance from him. "I'm not sure what I could possibly do that would be of assistance, Senna. You've got contacts and skills..."

"I need someone on the ground. Someone who can keep their eyes open and let me know if they hear or see—"

Tension seeped into every pore. Was she considering some kind of mutiny? "On who?" He couldn't help the blunt words.

"Not on Jonah or Daniella, if that's what you're thinking." Her lips tightened. "But when you're out, off base and on missions. I need intel on a finding I made today. Jonah knows, but I think it's the tip and something big is heading this way. Something that could put us all in a great deal of danger, and the base. Like more than we're currently in. With the colony ships so close... Look, I don't want to discuss it here." She slipped the spoon into the mush. "This is disgusting."

He shook his head, wondering if she'd say anything else, but instead she ate. Methodically. Scoop, chew, swallow, and repeat.

When they'd both finished, he waited. Well aware she wanted something from him. *Likely not the same thing as I'd like.*

"Let's take a walk. I need to clear my head a little, see what other aspects I've missed of this." She shook her head, and he couldn't help noticing the cloud of chocolate-colored silk which escaped the savagely taut ponytail on the top of her head.

What has she discovered? Hopefully, she'd share all soon. He stood, and she followed suit.

"Well, that was a meal experience," she said.

He trailed her to the front door. "Something like that," he murmured.

The girl cleaning the tables scurried forward as they left the building.

"So, you wanted to tell me something," he spoke carefully once they'd traveled a distance from earshot of others.

"I discovered what the compound was. Have you ever heard of triacetone triperoxide?"

"No, but judging from your concern, I'd say it's dangerous, in the wrong hands, and potentially an issue for us?" He jammed his hands into his pockets.

"You're much quicker than you appear, Mann. But then, I should have known better given who you hung around with during the combat phase. This explosive is a compound that's super-unstable and super-efficient at blowing stuff up. The only thing is, it's also pretty close to undetectable, I think, from what I've been able to research. Jonah is organizing Maylin to get me onto the ultranet system without being networked to any of the other systems so I can delve deeper and get a better idea."

He held up a hand and stopped her, startled to realize she didn't know what they already had in place. "We've already got one. I guess Jonah didn't know because we skated under the radar. We arranged that before Liv... Before we found out she was basically an infiltrator and she nearly killed Erin."

"What?"

Her startled glance informed him he'd somehow told her something she hadn't been apprised of. "You did hear about the Liv situation, or were you on mission at the time?"

Senna nodded, brows drawn close as if she were frustrated. "Yes, I know about Liv, but what do you mean infiltrator?"

He sighed. *How much to tell?* Franklin cleared his throat. "Okay, so Liv, or LV-1 as was her designation, had pretty much free range after Jonah and Daniella took her under their wing. We were hoping she'd be the bridge between us and the kids we'd rescued. Seems she was a plant, and those in charge of the kids were sure we'd be unable to refuse her... I guess, citizenship." His shoulders rose and fell in a shrug. "They probably thought we'd be weaker by giving into our emotions. So, Liv had full run and was basically a member of the family. She betrayed us, nearly killed Erin after pushing her down the stairs and after we became aware that she'd been hacking into the system. Sometime during all this, Maylin organized a bank of stand-alone units for us to research and run ID scans while we were looking into who was passing intel to the warrior children."

Her lips curved upward. "Franklin Mann, you've just made my day, and I could kiss you. Hell, hold on." She reached over, clasping her hands on either side of his head, and her lips collided with his.

The sound—a loud and echoing smack—started a slow burn began deep in his belly.

Senna stilled, her eyes glinting in the half-light. "Well now, I didn't expect that." Instead of her robust voice, a husky quality had settled in its place.

He harrumphed. The way his body responded wasn't anything he'd planned to act on. "Well, it's probably one of those things. Like eating in the mess."

But Senna didn't laugh. Instead, she frowned. "Franklin, I'm not the kind of woman who believes in footloose behavior, but neither am I a saint who lives in isolation. That kiss was unusual. Under normal circumstances, I'd be keen to investigate any kind of opportunities that may arise, but clearly you're not interested, so—"

Now he sputtered. "I'm a simple man, Senna. What you see is exactly what you get. Hand-to-hand combat, sniper, and bodyguard. I'm not an officer, nor am I the kind of guy who—"

"Mann, if I asked you straight out, are you a good soldier, you'd say yes, right?"

The interruption stopped him in his tracks. He considered her words. "Yes."

"You follow orders, right?"

Franklin couldn't help but nod.

"So why then, if I told you to list your best qualities, do I get the feeling you'd rather list your worst?"

Now Franklin laughed, though it was somewhat strangled. "Because I'm not the man someone like you would—"

"Someone like me?" Iciness chilled her tone, stopping him abruptly.

He blinked slowly. *Shit! I offended her.* He closed his eyes, making a point to consider his words before speaking again. "I just meant, you're gorgeous, bright, and clever. An arson investigator, while I'm nothing special."

Her eyes glinted. "I don't like being told that my interest is flawed. I don't care if you're not sure you're anything special. I trust my instincts. They've kept me alive for a long time."

Bitterness coated her words, and the chill he'd felt became a frigid blast, cutting right through to his guts.

She continued. "It led me to the discovery of the triacetone triperoxide. It tells me you're a good soldier and probably a nice person. What it didn't tell me is that you'd duck rather than admit my interest in you is unwelcome. All you had to do is say 'no thanks'." Senna backed away, hands stretched out between them. "But hey, now I've learned my lesson and won't bother you again."

How did that unravel so fast? His head spun, and he wanted to tell her it wasn't that he was a coward, just pure truth, but in her eyes he saw a world of ice that now ran between them and decided he should keep his mouth shut.

She spun on her heel, marched a couple of steps, then whirled back. "I'll meet you at the commander's office tomorrow at 0800 hours. And Mann? Don't be late."

Senna stalked away, leaving Franklin wondering how she'd battered him black and blue with simple words.

*B*ack in her room, Senna sank onto the bed. Franklin Mann, she mused, had pushed buttons she'd forgotten about tonight, and she'd over-reacted. Big time. The thing was, she'd seen him in the past. He might be a huge chunk of a man, he'd also proved more than once that he could be soft and gentlemanly.

"I guess that's why I took the chance," she muttered.

She tore off her shirt, once more investigating the scars that crisscrossed her torso and shoulders. The scars she'd gained as a prisoner-of-war. The reason she'd left the military.

The bottle of ointment she'd stashed on the table beside the bed had become part of her nightly routine, so Senna reached for it, twisted the lid off, squirted some into her hands, and rubbed it into the marred flesh.

What would Franklin Mann make of these? Would he be disgusted and turn away, or would he ignore them? Even more, would he touch them, accept them as part of who she was?

"Well, I probably won't ever know now." And that chilled her center in a way she'd been wholly unprepared for.

Shucking the rest of her clothes, she pulled on the light cotton robe she preferred to sleep in, stashed her discarded uniform, and crawled into bed.

Tomorrow was another day.

CHAPTER 4

Franklin Mann strode across the parade grounds, well aware he'd arrive dead on time, and snorted. "That's a stupid thought."

He'd passed an indifferent night, wondering if there was some way he could soothe over the mess he'd made with Senna, so being up early, washing clothes and straightening his rooms kept him busy. Then he'd waited, impatiently, knowing precisely how long it took to cross the base to Jonah's office.

The whole time his mind had churned over the conversation from the night before. He had the greatest respect for Senna and found her attractive, but after that discussion, any hopes he may have harbored were well and truly dead. Not that he had any expectations they'd be any more than working partners—no matter what she said, he was still nowhere near her league—but if they were going to have to spend time together, then he needed to soothe her down.

He knew exactly what that meant. He'd seen Michael with his sister and later Clarissa, enough to understand the politics of relationships, or at least on a cursory level.

Shaking his head, he entered the building, marveling at how much restoration work had been done since the explosion here mere weeks ago.

At the end of the corridor, Jonah was talking with a staffer, so he waited. When Jonah was done, Franklin advanced. "They've done a good job. You'd hardly know the building was attacked mere weeks ago."

"Yes. But we have a bigger problem. Is Senna here yet?" Jonah growled.

Franklin kept his face passive, hoping Jonah wouldn't notice the lack of enthusiasm for the meeting ahead. "I don't think so."

Jonah squinted. "And what's happened to make you button down, bro?"

Franklin sighed. "Personal stuff." He hoped it would throw Jonah off the scent.

"Ah. Well, been there, done that. If you need advice..."

"Thanks, man." A surge of relief swept over him as the door opened and Senna stepped inside.

"Good. Sorry I'm late, Jonah, I got a tag from someone in the arson squad who thought they'd heard I was, as he put it, 'sniffing around' the hospital. He was reminding me I'm still on suspension." She screwed up her face, and Franklin had the feeling it was more than frustration that caused her reaction.

"Ahh. You didn't tell him—"

"Fuck no, Jonah. What they don't yet know won't hurt them. But Franklin said last night that Maylin had an off-radar system. One that was used after the Liv incident."

Jonah winced, and Franklin read Senna's surprise at the action, then her embarrassment.

"Oh... Sorry," she mumbled, a tide of red cresting her cheeks.

Jonah sighed. "No. It's right. She took us all in, and we should have been more careful. Are now. I didn't know about the system, but if it's already in place, we should utilize it. Where is it located?"

"The infirmary lab," Franklin answered, his gaze settled on the commander, looking for a hint that he'd been unbalanced by the reminder of his almost adopted daughter's actions.

"Ahhh... One of those? All right, how much time do you need, because this is tight. I've got the colony ship almost ready for launch. We're going to need to bring in the families in the next couple of days, and it needs to be handled with strike precision."

Jonah turned away, rubbing a hand through his hair, and not for the first time, Franklin thought how the commanding of men seemed to be a perfect fit for his friend.

"Depends what I can find today. I'll need to drill down, then if I can find a sniffer, work out either how we can make one or scare something up."

"We've got three days before I need you ready for duty on the craft. We can't afford for the children to get wind of it, so Franklin, get Maylin in on the process. I need the unit and searches cloaked. I want updates as soon as you have them, and since today is Monday, I'll need you back here Wednesday morning 0600 for a briefing. That's all I can give you, Senna. Franklin, you're good to assist?"

"Well, I—" He didn't really want to, but Jonah was already nodding.

"He's perfect, Jonah. We'll get out of your hair." Senna turned and was through the door before Franklin could make his feet move.

"Franklin? You could have your hands full there."

Franklin shrugged. "I don't think I'd even get a chance. Things being what they are—"

"Take it from your old pal, love makes crazy bedfellows, but it's worth the shot."

Jonah turned and entered his office, leaving Franklin staring at the door. *If only it were that easy.*

Senna stared at the machine. "This?"

Maylin laughed, a tinkle. "I've tweaked it a little. And I've got some special software installed. All I need to know is your chosen search strings and *voila!*" The little Asian woman made a circle with her hands, but Senna simply gazed at her.

The machine was *ancient!*

Maylin growled, "Don't look like that. What you see on the surface isn't the same as what's beneath the hood, you know. Now, first string."

Senna rattled off the selected words, then watched as Maylin entered them into a software program she'd never seen before. "Who wrote that?" She wondered aloud, and Maylin loosed another tinkle.

"Me. After the Liv incident—"

Senna groaned. "Why does Liv come up in every sentence?"

Maylin settled down in the seat Senna had been avoiding. "You haven't been as involved in the more personal aspects of the fight. I know you're new to the team and all. Liv was Jonah and Daniella's sort of adopted daughter. She was also one of the first to be found and repatriated—or so we thought. I think Clarissa was hopeful that a child with the bio-engineering and who'd been indoctrinated would be saveable." Maylin punched some words into the computer as she explained the situation. "Daniella and Clarissa took it hard. I think they both had hopes that we could rehabilitate those they find. It just proved to them that you couldn't trust these children."

Senna hadn't realized how deep the commitment to Liv had been. Sure, she'd seen the child on the base, and Franklin had told her that it was a committed relationship from both adults involved, but she hadn't really understood. At least, not until Maylin spelled it out like that.

"Okay, so maybe I need to be more aware of what happened previously. What about Clarissa?" Senna asked. "She seems okay."

Maylin snorted. "She's great, and you've probably worked out she's had extensive cybe-therapy like Michael?"

Senna nodded. "Yeah, you can't miss that. Her shining eyes kind of give it away."

"She was an unwilling lab rat. Colvert, the guy who took her and experimented on her, was the owner of the fertility clinics they used to make the implanted embryos. She escaped, but he'd done a job on her. Like messed with her head and everything. I think there were even thoughts that Liv may have been cloned from Clarissa's DNA or something similar."

Senna's mouth dropped open. "Oh my God. And Michael? What does he say?"

"Well, apart from the fact that Clarissa is perfect, if he'd been able to lay his hands on Colvert when they brought him in, there'd only be little pieces. But they needed him too much to be able to allow that. So instead, Colvert is being kept in a secured location. A *classified* location." Maylin grinned, and not for the first time, Senna shivered at that action. *This woman is downright scary!*

While Senna had been dealing with internal machination in the arson squad all this had been boiling away, and she hadn't known anything. In fact, the very knowledge that Jonah had kept this from her hurt because they'd been such close friends before.

"But you're new. From the arson squad, right? What brought you to this place?" Maylin's words dragged Senna's concentration back to the matter in hand.

Resting her gaze on Maylin, Senna considered the woman. She was a certified computer genius, but working with the military rather than the colony ships didn't make a lot of sense. "So why are you here, Maylin? You could be making a fortune on the colony ship project."

"I like the intrigue and cut and thrust. Plus, the military gave me my start in computer tech. I owe them."

"Jonah needed my expertise, and at that time, the arson squad had some issues. I was the newest and the only female," Senna offered in return for the candid answer from Maylin. "It's still a patriarchal system in there, and I was unwelcome. The last case I worked on, someone tampered with my findings and I was hauled before the board. They claimed I'd made a mess of my investigation, which I hadn't, but I was suspended indefinitely. The thing is, it was a case where I was dealing with—" Senna sucked in a deep breath, realization dawning. "Fuck me, I was dealing with the same compound."

Maylin jerked her way. "What? You need to advise Jonah."

"I will, just as soon as we see if there is anything useful on the ultranet."

A *ping* echoed, and Maylin swung back to the computer. "Take a look for yourself. I've had to dive through layers of security and encryption, but I think what you want is here."

Rolling the chairs to the right, Senna took up position at the screen. "Yeah, just what I need. Let's open the file and—"

Even as she reached out, Maylin swatted her hand away. "No. We access it through a re-routed system. If it's got a self-destruct tag, which I'm expecting it to, not only will it destroy the file, but also send a targeted worm at us. Just let me..." Maylin tapped away, muttering to herself, then slid back. "There, now the page is loading."

And it did. "An optoelectronic nose?" Senna scrolled down the page. "Can we remotely save this?"

When Maylin shook her head, she sighed.

"Okay, so I need to write down—"

Maylin laughed. "You can't save, but we can print. Hang on." She pressed another button, and the box behind her started the screech.

"What the fuck?" Senna sprang up and marched over. "Paper? This is really old tech!"

Maylin tinkled a laugh. "You'll survive, Senna."

As the printout completed, she bit her lip, scanned the data. "Now I need specs on how to build one. Can you find them too?"

Maylin rolled her eyes. "Need you ask?"

Minutes passed as Senna waited patiently. Eventually, Maylin sat back with a grin, and the box behind them that had ceased its chatter began again. When it finished, Maylin scooped up the papers and thrust them at Senna, who glanced over them.

"I've got most of the parts, Maylin. We can build one and test it if you have access to—"

"If you're missing things, I may be able to configure or print it out for you three dimensionally." Maylin shrugged.

Senna nodded. "I have fragments of things that we can cannibalize to create these boxes. We'll need a set for every team. How long do you think it would take? If I needed parts?"

The door burst open, and Franklin entered the room. "Sorry, I had to go with Michael on a quick patrol. We ran out of some medications he needed urgently."

Senna took a moment to fill herself with the view of the man who she'd foolishly treated poorly. He looked super-inviting. At six feet, he was the perfect height for them to nestle cheek to cheek. His short, dark hair against weathered, dark skin was incredibly masculine, while his dark chocolate eyes were the sort a woman could get lost in.

He was large, but not the muscle-bound of cover models, rather the tough-as-nails variety that came from hard work, and for a moment, she considered what he'd look like, shiny in the sun, coated in a layer of oil, and her mouth dried at the vision that rose.

"We've been quite successful, Franklin. Your girl Senna here is pretty on the money with her keywords, and we've managed to find specs for a nose that will sniff out the compound." Maylin grinned, and Senna wanted to duck out of sight.

His smile was tight, as if he held back his emotions on a rope. "Excellent."

Maylin looked from Franklin to her and back again. "Well, I'll take these specs back to my basement and see what my team and I can conjure up, shall I?"

"I'll need copies too," she called to Maylin's retreating back, aware that Franklin was watching her. "Frank, I—"

"Franklin. Everyone calls me Franklin."

Head tilted, she studied his face. The chiseled jaw and sharp cheeks. "Franklin, I acted like a dick last night. I don't know why, only to say that the kiss sort of short-circuited my brain."

She watched as his wide lips clamped harder, so white lines edged them.

"Franklin, I'm trying here." Senna fought the urge to squirm.

"Okay, so here goes. I'm a little intimidated by you, Senna. You've got it together, and I know it sounds like a cop-out when I say I'm not good enough, but honestly, you need someone who can match you. Your wits and—"

On a frustrated groan, Senna closed the gap between them,

grabbed his hands, and pulled him against her body. "You're a kind and caring guy, Franklin. One I'd like to get to know socially. Don't pull the 'you're better than me' crap, because I don't tolerate that rubbish easily. Okay?"

His eyes crinkled at the corner. "You like to talk bluntly, don't you?"

Senna shrugged. "Seems to me the other option is diplomacy, and I think it's safe to say that—"

The klaxon split the air, and Senna sucked in a deep breath. "We need to get out of here."

Franklin tugged her to the exit, his hand already unsnapping his MX-517 from its protective holster.

Senna cursed, realizing her tiny MIG-11 was in her lockbox. "Damn!"

He turned, eyes scanning for threats. "What?"

"I left my weapon in the lines."

A smile wreathed his face, and he pulled her into an alcove and bent down to lift one pant leg, exposing a calf holster containing a MIG-11. "You know this one, right?"

"Oh yeah. I have one just like it."

He shoved it into her hand. "If the base is under attack, stay behind me. I'm a bigger target, and it may just save your life."

"Screw that," she ground out. "I don't stand behind any man. So, move your ass."

Franklin blinked. The alarm meant they were under attack and everyone who wouldn't be shoring up the breach was to report to the commanders. He, however, was required to guard Michael, Clarissa, and other non-combatants. Including the many infants on the base.

"What duty were you assigned?" he asked Senna as they barreled around a corner.

"Non-combatants," she panted, her long legs eating up the ground they had to cover.

Franklin nodded. As the most senior guard positioned in that location, it was his duty to ensure the safety of those unable to fight. Perhaps if he placed her close to Michael, Clarissa, and baby Eliza, he could concentrate better. Meanwhile, he would be taking the position in the tower so he could see the battle and direct his teams to either disperse and cover the civilians or provide necessary backup if required.

"I need you with Clarissa, Michael, and the baby. Their protection is your main role."

"Wait!" she called as he peeled off, heading for the tower. "Where will you be?"

"In the tower. Go. Find them, keep them in the center, and be careful."

Franklin sprinted, heading for the tower, weaving through knots of gathered civvies who cried and huddled as they ventured to their designated locations. He watched as his men forced them into the center of the grounds and inside the infirmary, then took up position around them. As they'd drilled, the babies were protected in the middle along with their medical staff.

At the base of the tower, he sent one last glance in the direction of Senna's location then put her out of his mind as he shoved his rifle strap over his head. It crisscrossed his body, and he began the climb, arm over arm as legs found and used the ladder to propel him upward.

When he reached the top, he stopped and glanced in the direction of the noise. There was a gaggle of children at the gates, and he noted a plume of smoke, but it was the far edge that caught his attention. "Damn!"

Reaching for his communicator, he hailed Jonah.

"What?"

"Possible incursion to the north corner. I'd say they're attempting to concentrate your attention. Using it as a distraction while smaller numbers move at the edges of the eastern and southern boundaries.

The north corner is the greatest mass. They're attempting to get to the colony ships."

"Dammit. Can you lead a team there, put Senna on the tower as she hasn't the combat experience but is a clear head?"

"Will do."

There were a few men he'd need on the guard duty, and leaving Senna in control of the tower made sense, but his brain was ticking over the fact that they were dividing the teams into even smaller troops.

"We need more men," he muttered as he clambered down as quickly as possible.

"As soon as I can spare them, we'll reinforce you," answered Jonah, and Franklin broke the connection.

Finding the ground, Franklin shoved his way through the doors. Throngs of people gathered in the way and he shoved past them. "Senna!" he bellowed.

She appeared before him, her face a flat mask.

"I need you on the tower. Watching out for the movement of the children. We've got an attempted incursion on the northern corner, heading for the colony ship. I'm taking a group to defend."

Her face tightened. "But you don't have enough men to adequately protect—"

"We'll make do. Tower, now." He stepped away, looking left and right for Sevres, Fairburn, Alamede, and Sorrantes. As he rounded them up, he glanced and noted Frecklington, who he'd served with, and hailed him over. "Frecklington, stay with Michael, Clarissa, and the baby. Direct from in here. Senna is taking over on the tower."

Franklin's gaze narrowed while he considered the men waiting by the door, and he strode over to them.

"Follow me," he ordered.

They hotfooted across the base, hurdling bikes and anything else that lay discarded on the way.

"Northern corner, attempted incursion. Heading for the colony ships. Reinforcements coming soon, we just have to hold the line." His rifle bumped against his leg as he moved. Franklin couldn't spare the time to glance back to make sure they were keeping up. They needed speed to save the ships.

The whole time his mind spun, considering what he knew about the project, the children, and trying to work out how they'd advance. It would be sneaky. Underhanded. They'd need to employ guerilla tactics with so few men to cover the area. *We need our wits about us.*

"Sevres, Fairburn, take the left. Your job is to take out anyone who gets through with suppressive fire. Don't care about the age or gender. Just do the job while staying low. Whatever it takes, men. Alamede, I want you to take the nearest building. Hunker down and snipe away. Sorrantes, scare me up some flash-bangs. We're going to need them."

He checked his ammo pouches. Full. His knives were sharp, but he had a couple of extra items perfect for these kinds of skirmishes. He'd front them first, create confusion so his men could do their jobs.

He knew Sorrantes. The man had been a demon in a fight, cunning and inventive. Just what they needed right now.

Franklin glanced around the area, chose his location with care, more than a little aware that once Sorrantes began hurling flash-bangs he'd have to back off. "Just gotta buy everyone time," he muttered.

He patted at his pockets and dragged out a favorite up-close-and-personal tool. The gloves he retrieved were heavy, studded with lead on the top yet supple enough to still be able to use his gun and the knives he wore. These tactics would be brutal, but effective.

Next, Franklin tugged on the helmet, battered and scarred. He'd worn it during the war. But it was a necessary piece of equipment, mouth cover closing over the filtered breathing unit. Franklin considered, then he advanced to the spot he'd chosen, working his way along the barrier obscured by bushes. The wire would slow them down for a moment or two, depending on what equipment they carried.

Franklin heard them long before he saw them. They may be trained in aspects of warfare, but they missed some of the intrinsic values of silence in these situations. For a second, he wondered if that training was purposeful or through lack of experience and qualified trainers.

Their not quite fully developed voices raised, calling out actions that would probably confuse those opposing them. *I don't need to hear them to know what they're going to do.* His hands on the wire just beyond the bushes tugged and pulled until it started sagging. He waited a moment longer, letting them achieve a false sense of safety.

The flash of wire cutters propelled him into action.

Dashing out, he caught the nearest around the ankles in a lock, tugged the teen down and cuffed him. The teenager howled and bucked. Others turned, and he hefted the boy he'd just flattened, used him as a battering ram, shoving the others crowding around back.

The teen turned limp, and Franklin dropped the body as a rifle swung in his direction. Franklin dipped, turned, and it sailed millimeters from his head. His left arm moved, swooping in a wide circle, caught a boy of about fourteen in the chin, and down he went in a hail of blood and teeth.

Franklin grunted, all thought beyond survival melting back. Every move instinctual, he danced with those who came at him, cutting a swathe down the middle so what should be a cohesive unit splintered into two ragged groups.

In the teens' eyes he read hesitation and confusion.

Exactly what they needed.

The comm unit in his helmet squarked. "Flash-bangs on site."

He didn't turn, knowing his back would present an easy target. Move forward or retreat. Retreat was the best option, but he spied a child ahead. She looked exactly like Liv.

His gut curdled at the thought that Clarissa and Michael may also be facing her clone, and he took a step in her direction, her gaze superior and it fed the fury in his soul.

His senses otherwise occupied, he didn't see the gun butt, but felt the impact for a second as it crashed down on his head. Even though it glanced off the helmet, the reverberations echoed through his brain. Awareness compromised, he barely heard the sound of the device detonating.

Children fell around him, the sleeping gas infused flash-bang a quick and effective tool. Thankful for the breathing apparatus in his helmet and the ballistic material, he still fell back under the explosive action.

The sky and everything around him turned gray, then all disappeared.

CHAPTER 5

*S*enna fumed. What the hell was Franklin doing going into the center of a bunch of warriors in a hand-to-hand tussle on his own?

They'd brought him in, having fended off the attack, on a stretcher. He was still out cold, and for a moment, fear blossomed inside her. What if he'd sustained some as yet unknown injury and didn't wake up?

"He'll be fine when he comes to," Michael muttered after they'd removed Franklin's headgear. "No broken bones, but he'll likely have a concussion. Even now, he's starting to wake."

Waiting outside the door with Jonah and Daniella, who'd been touring the medical facility since the skirmish ended, wasn't exactly where she wanted to be.

The panic filling her made little sense. After all, she was the lone wolf girl. The one who went it alone. Didn't need or want anyone fussing over her.

Except this time, someone she liked had done exactly the same thing and come off second best.

"He'll be fine, Senna." Jonah placed his hand on her shoulder.

She wanted to remonstrate, to assure them that it was only because she could see friendship between her and the man currently unconscious in the room beyond that caused her to act out of character. The thing was, she couldn't quite bring herself to say the words aloud. Because they weren't true.

"We need to finish the rounds." Daniella steered her husband away from the doorway, but Senna continued to hover.

"Se... Senna?" She heard her name, and the knot of worry in her belly—the one she'd tried hard not to acknowledge—eased.

"She's just outside, slugger. Let me check you over and I can call her in if you like."

The door offered support as her limbs turned watery and her eyes burned.

"Now." Franklin's voice carried a steel undertone, and Senna wanted to both cheer and yell at him. Instead, she straightened up, rounded the corner, and looked at the bruised man lying on the bed.

"Well, you're a sight." Her voice almost sounded normal. Except for the squeak at the end.

Michael glanced at her as if reminding her that Franklin was a patient, but emotions warred inside her, jagged waves of panic edging out anything else.

"Sorry, Senna." Franklin reached for her, and for the first time, she noted the bloodied leather gloves studded with metal.

She tugged away. "What are they?"

Michael stalked around the bed. "Meant to get them off before. Just a moment." He assisted Franklin in removing them, showing his swollen and deeply bruised fingers and hands. He didn't move a muscle, not a flinch or even a hiss of pain, but she saw echoes of it in his eyes.

Michael dropped the gloves onto a tray, and she moved back in. "Why? Where did they come from?"

Franklin hissed this time as he shrugged. "They're a little something extra I picked up in the services. I knew things would be bad, and I needed every tactic I could lay my hands on. Had to buy time. Worked, did it?"

Her face tightened into a scowl, her muscles screaming. "Just. They had reinforcements on the way when a platoon from the southern barracks arrived. We've now got more prisoners, and one looks just like—"

"Liv?"

"I was going to say Clarissa, but yeah, I guess. That was the stupidest, most foolhardy move I've ever seen, Franklin. What the hell were you thinking?" She crowded in, needing to make the point.

"I'm a good soldier, Senna. I followed my orders. Saved lives today. The colony ships survived, didn't they?"

Michael harrumphed. "They didn't get past you to it. We think the plan was to get only a couple in, those who were particularly trained in aeronautics and engineering. We discovered as some of the children were awakened that they showed an aptitude. It seems along with the cloning, they're now training specific children with skills for those areas. We just have to hope that none show an aptitude for biological warfare."

Senna gulped. "That's not even worth joking about, Michael."

But when he raised his gaze to hers, she staggered back. "I wasn't joking."

Franklin watched the briefing from the wheelchair Michael had insisted on, but he felt stupid sitting there like some kind of baby.

"We've got reinforcements on the way. David and Erin have made contact with the ex-service personnel they dealt with previously. Daniella is pulling every string to get as many transported by air to the base to bolster our troops. We're days away from the launch of the first colony ship, and for some reason, the warrior children want to disrupt it. While it doesn't make sense, we have to focus on getting that safely off the ground. We have a payload of nearly six hundred civilians, one hundred and twenty military and medical staff to launch. Plus the captain and his crew. This can't go wrong, people." Jonah stalked around the room, scratching his head, and stared at the gathered personnel.

Franklin waited, Senna perched beside him like some kind of odd, avenging nurse who'd strike at anyone coming too close. Her reaction to his wounding was puzzling, as was her hovering. He'd never had that before and had no frame of reference.

"Do you need something?" she whispered as if she'd spent all her time focused on him.

"No. Just trying to think why the colony ships present as high on their target list."

Erin came running into the room. "I have it! I know why. We've just interrogated one of the teens, and they let slip that if they could gain control, they could not just halt our population of the planet, but also take direct control themselves. They're planning at not just wiping out humanity as it's been for centuries, but also growing their numbers. Expanding their dominion as she put it. Including the other planets."

The sound of shock rippled through the room, collective in the horror of what had just been revealed.

"Holy hell," Franklin whispered. "They want to wipe us out first, then do the same on other planets. And we haven't even made it to space yet."

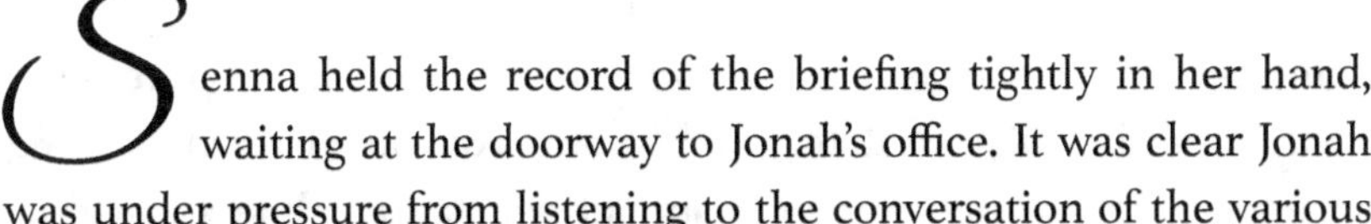

*S*enna held the record of the briefing tightly in her hand, waiting at the doorway to Jonah's office. It was clear Jonah was under pressure from listening to the conversation of the various commanders, rehashing what they'd learned during the briefing.

"We have to cut the head from the snake, Jonah. If they take control of the colony ship, humanity is unlikely to survive. We have to redouble the efforts to get those civilians up there. We'll need naval and air defense in place."

"Admiral, we have so many problems right now that this is the least of our concerns. We might have to postpone the launch until we have some of these things dealt with."

"We don't have time, Jonah. The forecasters aren't giving us a viable window of opportunity for more than the next month or so. And with the explosives expert you're going to bring in—and yes, I've heard of not just her rep, but also about who and what she is—let's be honest, if the compound is as volatile as—"

The door opened before Senna, and Jonah waved her inside to join the others in the meeting. "You know the gentlemen of course, don't you, Senna?"

She nodded. "Yes, sir."

"So, tell us about the compound. Is it as volatile as we've been led to believe?" the grizzled admiral demanded.

"It's incredibly unstable. Even on the shelf, which is why they used to call it the 'Mother of Satan'. It's archaic, and if it hadn't been for my introduction to it, and what I believe are their test sites—"

"Test sites? What do you mean?"

"Over the last six months I've come across several incidents where an explosive compound was indicated. However, it didn't match any currently known compounds. During my training this one was mentioned as a matter of course, part of an introduction and history briefing." She let that sink in while she scanned the room. Faces stared at her. Some wide with shock while others hunched forward, thinking over the importance of her words. "We do know there are ways to handle it. For instance, there is a way to include it into a putty-like substance. This way it gives it some form of easier handling, but as it's made from components that can be purchased easily, it's difficult to detect, and none of our current testing sequences are attuned..." Senna spread her hands while shrugging. "It's only because I showed an interest in it, researched it, and discovered a way to detect it after the fact that I was able to draw a conclusion on the sites I investigated."

"So what went wrong with your last case?"

Icy waves dashed over her, but she faced the admiral's gaze, aware of what he was asking. "My results were, in my opinion, tampered with. I kept detailed logs of my work, which I backed up to my home unit. My worksite was accessed and certain key facts deleted before they could be presented. Facts that remained on my personal unit from my manual backup process. When I was carpeted, I explained that and was accused of falsifying my backup files. I was further informed that on inspection no record of unauthorized entry into my files could be found. As a result, I was suspended, pending further investigation."

The admiral nodded slowly, no doubt considering her answers. "And you're sure this time..."

"I ran the tests on my mobile unit. I've also been investigating a way to track the explosives and believe this device we're currently manufacturing will be able to determine aspects of the explosive. In the history books, I was able to find a record of a device called an optoelectronic nose. It works by using general sensors for odors and volatile organic compounds. We apply a thin film of dye that is responsive to chemicals, allowing the nose to see the hints of the compounds. The nose detects their presence by using an array of multiple dyes whose colors change based on the full range of inter-molecular reactions to the substance we apply."

At the blank looks on their faces, she sighed.

"Each compound has a responsive color attached, right? We're looking for a specific filter, so we only apply that to the nose. It reacts on a molecular level. As every chemical has its own independent molecular structure, that's what becomes its weakness and what we employ to detect the compound," she explained.

The admiral steepled his hands and harrumphed. Silence stretched out before he cleared his throat again. "How long until you have it ready?"

Senna jostled from leg to leg, because there was no definitive answer she could give them. "It's hard to say. Maylin has the majority of the equipment required. I've got samples, so we can create the filter, but we have to be exact. We could get lucky and have it finalized in under a week, given we found a diagram and specs, but on the other hand, we still have to test it then fine-tune it."

"Sergeant Reed, we don't have time for fine-tuning." The admiral rose. "This is a step forward, but the warriors are getting bolder in their attacks. We barely held them off from their attack on the colony ships."

Her stomach lurched at the memory of Franklin being carried past her to the infirmary.

"We have to get that first ship off safely, otherwise I'm not sure we'll get another chance. They want it and we have it. Along with a responsibility to humanity. Time is of the essence." The admiral pushed away from the table, driving home his point that time was running short.

And boy, didn't she feel that as all gazes settled on her? The pounding in her head was second only to the pressure on her chest, and it took will to expand her lungs and suck in oxygen. "Sir, I'll do my best, but it's such old tech we don't have it on the shelf."

"Don't give me problems. Give me answers, Reed." The admiral's canny eyes bored right to her center, and there was nothing for it but to nod. "Go to Maylin. See how she's getting on then return for a full briefing at 1300 hours," the admiral demanded.

Jonah ushered her to the door. He held the door wide, and Senna stepped through before whirling back. "There aren't any shortcuts here, gentlemen. It has to be right. We'll do our best, but..." There really wasn't anything more to say, so she stepped away at Jonah's nod and closed the door.

Franklin stretched in the bed, still a little stiff, but ready for release from the infirmary. "Come on, doc. Let me out."

Michael leaned against the doorjamb. "If I do, you'll just go back out there and do something unwise. So, unless I release you to someone, who I know will keep you occupied, I'm not letting you out."

This isn't going the way I planned. He needed to get out before he went stir-crazy. Erin and David were currently in the middle of inter-rogations, but he wouldn't be much use to them. Jonah and Daniella were locked into meetings with various officials, and he wouldn't be much use to them either, and Michael and Clarissa were under the pump with the infants and casualties. Maylin ran circles around him with her computer talk, and Sevres and Fairburn were assisting David and Erin. All that left was…

"How about release me to Senna? She's working on some special project for Jonah, and you know she doesn't strike me as someone who'll let me do what isn't allowed." He controlled his smirk, sure Michael would accede, and once clear, well, if things got hectic and he was needed elsewhere…

"Not until I check with her to see what you'd be doing. Your body took a pounding, Franklin. Cracked ribs, concussion, and deep bruising. As your physician, I'm saying no. As your friend, I'm telling you that your body is like an instrument—it can and will break if you mistreat it."

Oh yeah, he'd heard this song before. "But I'm needed—"

"David and Erin went back to Homewoods. They've got reinforcements arriving tomorrow. Some seasoned and some newer recruits, so the pressure is off for the moment."

Homewoods. The small settlement David and Erin had found once their copter was compromised. David told them how it was filled with families of military personnel who'd been unable to return to society, damaged by what they'd seen and done.

"So how many did we lose in the attack?"

Michael bowed his head. "Five. But they lost twenty-two and we took nineteen more as prisoners. Among them was LV-3."

"Damn." He couldn't suppress the word, and Michael murmured his agreement. "I'm willing to help with the interrogation, if it would assist." It wasn't something he was overly skilled at, but he'd do whatever was necessary.

Michael grunted. "I doubt you'd be useful to them. More likely you'd scare the kids or beat them to a pulp." Michael's smile was grim. "I'll get onto Senna, and you're to stay here. And to make sure you do…" Michael beckoned someone forward, and in trod Clarissa, cradling baby Eliza. "…you're going to babysit."

"Ah, really?"

Clarissa grinned. "Not pleased to see me? I even brought you some food." Handing the baby to Michael, she reached around the corner and waved a bowl in the air. "Oats. With honey."

His stomach gurgled. "That's cruel."

She laughed. "Maybe, but Michael needs you to stay here, resting, until he's sure you won't injure yourself further. He worries about you."

Michael made a sound somewhere between a snort and a remonstration. "I wouldn't go—"

"Michael?" At Clarissa's tone, a red crest shined on his friend's face.

He almost laughed, until Clarissa pinned him with a glare. "Don't you dare, Franklin Harris Mann."

"Yes, ma'am," they both agreed.

"Good. Now, here's Eliza." Sliding the meal to the rolling table, she reached back and scooped the baby from her husband's grasp and placed her in Franklin's arms. "She's going to need her bottle as soon as you're done eating. Call me, and I'll be back to change her."

"You're not staying?"

"No. I have things to see to." Clarissa whirled and left him with Michael while he cradled the baby with one arm.

"Michael," he implored, but the other man simply shook his head.

"No way. My wife scares me." On a chuckle, Michael turned and left Franklin with the baby.

CHAPTER 6

Senna entered the infirmary and found Michael waiting for her in the foyer. "So, you're releasing Franklin into my care?"

"Only if you can keep him quiet. The bruising and cracked ribs will heal quickly with the regen I've applied, but he needs to rest. The body can't easily regain its strength without it. No lifting, no training, and absolutely no vigorous exercise. Since you're working on that sniffer project, there should be no reason for Franklin to be doing anything taxing."

"Okay." Senna wasn't sure she really wanted him hanging around her full time. It might get in the way of her actually doing her job, because she'd have the added distraction of his presence.

On the other hand, she'd have an assistant to help her check the progress of the filters. She already knew which chemical compounds highlighted the triperoxide. If she could come up with one that worked with the acetone as well, that would be gold.

She trailed Michael down the corridor to the room.

"No exertion, Senna," he admonished, and she nodded.

"Yeah, I get it." Then Senna entered the room, Michael retreating to annoy some other poor patient, she guessed. "Okay, Frank. Time to up and out. You're my prisoner for the next day or two, at least until the doc releases the reins."

He scowled. "I could go home. And the name's Franklin."

Her snort was inelegant, but it got his attention. "Yeah, I don't think so." She reached down and flipped back the bedcovers. "Up and at it, boy."

A glint settled in his eyes. "Oh, I could."

The words lanced her, a frisson of awareness starting at the timbre of his voice.

She stepped back. "I'll wait outside for you to dress," she said, aware the whole time that her nerves jumped in response to his casual comment.

In the corridor, with the door shut, she leaned back, hands resting on her belly, eyes closed. *Oh Lord. At least two days, and that voice...his presence. What am I going to do? He brushed me off, now he's playing. Focus! It's all about the work now.*

Too bad her libido refused to listen to her brain, because parts of her body had already heated to mush.

When the door opened, she'd regained some of her equilibrium, and she ushered Franklin in the direction of the nurse's desk to sign him out, then led him out into the sunshine. "We'll drop by your rooms so you can change, then onto the lab and Maylin."

"So, what do you want me for, exactly? And you're working with Maylin?"

Senna shook her head. There'd been too many incursions into sections of the base to be sure it was safe to talk freely. And after the story of the Liv incidents, she wasn't sure the infirmary was the best place to discuss strategy anyway. "Not here. Let's get you changed out of that dirty, stained uniform, and we'll grab a coffee somewhere quiet. Then I'll explain."

They moved at a leisurely pace. Franklin wanted to move faster and made frustrated sounds while she kept her gait shorter than usual. Clearly, he understood that she would ensure he followed orders while with her, and he kept his stride length equal to hers.

Senna waited outside as he popped inside the unit, and when he returned in a fresh uniform, she led him to a courtyard she'd discovered after they'd detoured to one of the small coffee dispenser units dotted around the base. The grassy area wasn't surrounded by buildings and gave a clear and uninterrupted view for a distance she considered safe.

"All right then. Tell me now," he said.

Senna settled on the seat and waited as he dropped down beside her. "You know about the photoelectronic nose in principle. The thing is, it has to have a marker to check the compounds against to work. The 'sniffing' is in fact a visual process. We already have a chemical signature for the triperoxide value, what we don't have is a signature that will work for both triperoxide and triacetone together. Not effectively. So, over the next couple of days, while they finish the colony ships and Maylin is building the device with her team, you and I will be working on finding a filter that fits for both. We only have days, because Jonah insists we check the ship before they load up. After that, we do the same process for the cargo, because nothing can be allowed to slide through. But we've only got limited time to finish this pre-work. As in three days."

Franklin stared at her. "But you have a signature that works with the triacetone, right? Why not just mix the triperoxide and triacetone sniffers together?"

"That's the thing, we might be able to, but we need to recreate the environment and the chemical in order to test what we come up with. Simply putting them together isn't necessarily the answer, because we can't be sure what changes the chemical might undergo once mixed in its raw state. I'm working off samples that have already exhausted their life. Add to that, I've been unable to find sources or information on how they created the filter for triacetone triperoxide. They're all locked down, and we haven't been able to break the encryption. Besides which, we don't have the time to research. We have to be doing stuff now."

"So, what's our first priority then?"

"Recreate the compound in a safe environment. We have to work quickly, because once the mixture is made, it's volatile. Unstable.

Then we use the filters we've created. We need to make up a range of filters pretty much at the same time, fit them to the nose once Maylin is finished, then test them. Here's where I need your assistance. I need someone to prepare everything so I can run the checks. I need a location to work, preferably off the base."

Franklin gazed at her, eyes wide open. "You're mad."

"No, just desperate."

"I can't think of... Hell, I can actually." His skin assumed a pallor and a line of beaded sweat stood out on his upper lip. For a moment, Senna wondered if she was pushing too much and too hard. "Michael will explode once he knows. But to use this location we're going to need backup."

She perked up at his words. "Where?"

Franklin shoved his hands deep into his pockets, looking worried, creases forming on his brow. "The lab where they experimented on Clarissa. It's in a remote location. The labs haven't yet been picked apart. There are blast-resistant workrooms, and we can lock it down from the interior. Jonah, Michael, and I investigated it after we found Clarissa."

"That would be perfect, except we'd need to get there, be assured of safety. Once I begin work with this stuff, we can't afford any interruptions. People will die if this goes wrong, Franklin."

"We need a couple of others to back us up, I agree. Security we can trust will be essential."

Senna nodded. "We need to check in with Maylin, see how much longer she needs, then collect the necessary equipment and chemicals. Then we have to hope like hell we get lucky, because if we don't, I can't be assured of the safety of all these people on the base. Their lives and deaths, if we don't get this right, will haunt me forever."

Franklin didn't like the responsibility being shoved onto Senna's shoulders. Too little time and far too much responsibility for a single person usually led to mistakes. He just had to hope it didn't come to that.

They hurried to Maylin's workroom, which was hidden in a basement. She met them at the door.

"Franklin, good to see you on your feet again. Now, Senna, the specs were a little light on in a couple of areas, but my team is the best, and they've made some alterations which will increase the battery life, and the sensitivity we believe you may require. We've also made the filter slides larger, so you'll get a better reading."

Senna took the proffered machine. "You're sure?"

Maylin drew herself up to her full height of just over five foot. "I don't say anything I don't mean, Senna. My team worked night and day. We've ratted through essential equipment to scavenge the parts required, so yes, I'm sure."

The crest of red on Senna's cheeks were a surprise. "Of course. Thanks, Maylin. Can you create a few more? If this works, we're going to need a team to check the target. It's too big for one person."

"Already working on it. Once we hear from you on the efficacy of the machine, we'll swing into production. Should be able to finish three in the next week, and just have them at tweak point in case something needs refining."

Franklin watched the two women stash the ugly but sensitive items into a padded container.

"I'll take that." He reached for it, but Senna brushed his hand away.

"No, you won't, Franklin Mann," Senna said. "You're my assistant, not slave. And besides, you're not allowed to carry or lift." Maylin tittered and Senna smiled. "Thanks, Maylin. I'll be in touch."

Franklin seethed on the way to the vehicle. "I'm not an invalid," he groused once she'd eased into the driver's seat.

"Maybe not. But my orders were clear, and I'm not going to face Michael and say I ignored them to save your manhood." The click of the safety belts echoed in the now silent vehicle.

There really wasn't any use in arguing, he decided. She was just as hard-headed as his friend, so he merely watched as she ignited the engine and pulled away from the curb.

Senna arrived at Franklin's coordinates and simply stopped outside the large, white building. It looked like a prison. The tall structure was cold and impersonal.

"You're sure this is it?" Senna asked. As she turned, she caught sight of the taut planes of Franklin's face.

"Yeah. This is where the bastard held Clarissa for over six months. It's where they impregnated her, cut her up, and implanted the cybectronic parts. The bastard was only three miles from town and got away with murder. We found the remains of several other victims of his therapies."

"It should have been demolished, though I'm grateful for the lab space." She spoke vicously now, her tone hard and sharp like a knife.

"Wait until you see inside. Then tell me that." His words were stones that tugged at her brain. What else could possibly be in there to compound the realities they already knew?

"Has it been fully investigated?"

"There wasn't time or resources. The warrior kids were coming out of the woodwork, and we had to abandon our homes for the security of the base."

Senna pushed an errant lock of hair out of her eyes. "What about on the other continents though. Are things as bad there?"

"We've only received minimal reports. But yes, for the most part, the same has happened worldwide. Some of the more remote southern continents don't have the same issues, but that's more because the terrain isn't conducive to their advance at this time."

She'd half-expected his answers, but hearing the brutal truth made her wonder if there was any chance of overcoming the threat to them all. *Are we fighting without any chance of winning?* She shook her head against that self-defeatist thought.

Senna drove forward, glancing left and right for any indication they'd been detected or that the lab was breached. At the secure garage, they alighted. Senna grabbed the lockbox and her small satchel containing the offcut she'd taken from the hospital site and her notes.

At the front she waited for the team who'd traveled ahead to open the access door, while her body quivered with tension.

If there were combatants out there, this was the time they'd attack, in her estimation. Hairs on the nape of her neck upended and she half-turned as the door opened. Senna gave her full attention to the man beyond. In the region of maybe his middle-fifties, the man took pains with his appearance. His gray-flecked, dark hair was short, and his body was as toned as a twenty-year-old's.

"Sevres," acknowledged Franklin as the man waved them inside.

"Be quick, Franklin."

"No issues?" he asked the man before him, but Sevres shook his head.

The door slid shut with a whoosh and the low buzz of the security lockdown sounded.

"Show me to the lab." Senna repositioned the bag on her shoulder, felt the weight shifting, and changed her stance accordingly.

"This way."

Sevres led them from the wide foyer through swinging doors. "The walls and doors of this place are reinforced. They'd need a missile to gain entrance." Footsteps echoed in the silence, and a musty smell from disuse clogged her nostrils.

"How long has the place been empty?"

"Since Clarissa. About a year or so," Sevres answered.

Lights above her head flickered, and she detected signs of mold and mildew growth. She just hoped the lab was cleaner, otherwise she'd have work to attend to before she began setting up for the experiment.

The further within the building they traveled, the more unsure she became. The corridor reminded her of the ancient horror movies they played in the wee hours of the night, darkly forbidding, and each door they passed was a chilling reminder of what this building had been.

They reached a door and Sevres pushed it open. The room contained everything she'd need, but it required urgent cleansing.

"Ah, damn," she muttered.

Franklin moved in front of her. "What's wrong?"

"We'll need to clean before I can begin. Every surface wiped down and a clean room established. Any speck of dust or grime will compromise our outcomes. We need to find the utility room and get cleaning."

Sevres and Franklin looked at her as if she were mad.

"What? Haven't you ever cleaned before?" If the situation weren't so dire, she'd almost laugh. "If there are others, get them down here and we can have this sorted in a matter of hours."

"I... Of course, Sergeant Reed."

Sevres shot through the door, likely heading off to contact the others, and Franklin grinned. "I didn't expect this, but whatever you want, Senna."

If it were a matter of whatever I wanted, then that would be— She cut the thought off before it went any further. Now wasn't the time to be considering that kind of rot, Senna told herself.

CHAPTER 7

The cleaning wasn't exactly enjoyable, though it was cathartic, Franklin admitted privately. Senna was adamant that he shouldn't do any lifting or excessive turning, instead finding him a stool at a large sink and setting him to washing the droppers and test tubes.

"I can do more," he argued much to Senna's obvious frustration.

"Michael will skin me alive if you hurt yourself, and these need a thorough cleansing before I can use them. I'm going to set up the centrifuges and burners."

Senna stalked off, and he took a moment to watch the unconscious sway of her hips and the long lines of her body. Lean and strong. Well-honed and very unlike the women he'd dated in the past. He'd preferred curvy and well-rounded at hip and breast. A woman who could carry out a rational conversation, it was true, but the body had always been just as important.

He returned his thoughts to the task at hand. The boxes she'd dumped beside him appearing never-ending initially. As the time passed, he worked methodically, the drying racks she'd set out at the beginning filling with the glass equipment. Franklin listened to the chatter in the room.

"I wasn't sent here to clean," groused one of the guards.

Franklin almost laughed, as neither was he, but this was the task she needed completed before she could begin her work.

"Complaining again, are you?" He heard Senna demand and smothered his sputter of amusement.

"Er, no, sergeant," the man answered, and Franklin swallowed a laugh at the chastened answer the man gave Senna.

Hands on her hips, Senna towered over the man, her eyes glinting in the artificial light and her voice echoing in the cavernous chamber. "And for the record, no, I don't have a completed degree in science, but what you should be asking yourself is, if I don't get this done, and the room is compromised so the results are skewed, how will that affect the scanner? Will it work or cause the deaths of hundreds of civilians on the colony ship? Do I have enough knowledge of what I'm doing to save these people, and if I fail because of your interference, will you be able to sleep at night? So, don't whine. Just do what I've set out for you. None of us want to be here, but it's the price of saving millions of lives."

The man looked shamefaced and muttered, "Of course," and his mates gave him a wide berth for the rest of the day.

"I didn't know you'd studied science," Franklin whispered.

"I didn't finish my degree, because I didn't have the necessary funds to finish, so the guards seemed the best option. Afterward, returning to study with a bunch of fresh-faced, adult-kids made no sense. Instead, I joined the arson squad, used my knowledge there, and that's how I got here."

He wanted to ask her other questions, but she turned away. He had the impression it was a part of her life she didn't really want to discuss. But he could certainly tell that she was turning the memories over in her mind. He'd bide his time. Perhaps one day, she'd share.

Senna bustled around, cleaning the benches while others attacked the floors and walls until everything shined with a brilliant ceramic white. The burners she attached to the gas lines were in place, and the centrifuges were set up on another table. She raided the cupboards, and dispensed lab coats, gloves, masks, and even head coverings. Franklin watched as she crowed with glee after she located a stash of disposable items.

"Whatever we don't use, I'll take back to the base with me," she muttered aloud.

Setting up the items on the table, she checked over the provisions. "We need to keep the work area clear from contamination." Then she hefted the locked box onto the table beside her.

The latches clicked open, and Franklin saw her reach in and retrieve the precious scanner.

It didn't look like anything special, a two-piece set of hand-held units, a bit like a communicator base station, and a pair of glasses.

"What a find," murmured Senna, who then proceeded to explain how the item came equipped with a film slide attachment. "We'll use it to detect the compounds via the beam of light sent by the other half of the unit." The eyepiece, wireless and compact, she wore like spectacles.

"What do you need me to do?" he asked.

Senna shook her head. "There isn't much else right now. I need to make a test of the compound and apply it to some rocks. Maybe you should report back to base that we're set up? They may have some things they want you to retrieve."

He retreated, leaving her to work in silence. Once on the other side of the doors, he scooped up his communicator, one they'd fitted with a blocker, so no one else could hear their conversations.

"We're all go," he informed Jonah, and in the background he spied Daniella, the senator.

"Good. Look, unless you're needed, Daniella and I are aware the building was searched briefly then secured and abandoned, but if you can find any records, details about people, files we need to know. Anything that can give us a clear indication of Colvert's knowledge of the structure of our opponents will assist."

"In other words, you want a deep search and seize?"

Jonah nodded. "Information is power, and right now, we have a vacuum. I need people, places, and who did what. Anything that can give us an upper hand. Oh, and while you're at it, tell Senna to hurry. The engineers green-lighted the ship three hours ago."

Shit! Green-lighting the ship meant time now had almost run out. "She said it could take days."

"I can give her no more than forty-eight hours, Franklin. We need to inspect and load. We're out of time and options."

"I'll let her know and gather some men to check the building over."

"Good work, and thanks, Franklin." The line disconnected from Jonah's end, and Franklin shoved the communicator in his pocket.

Looking through the round glass portal on the door, he could see Senna bent over her work, so he decided to find some others and begin the search of the building. He'd apprise her later of his conversation with Jonah.

They settled on a room by room pattern. The therapy rooms were overwhelming with machines and cords, and none of them looked remotely like anything he'd seen in the infirmary.

They hauled all the comps out, packing them into boxes to take to the base once they were on their way back, well aware he hadn't the expertise himself and clearly no one on the taskforce here did either. Better to let Maylin at it than trip some hidden link that would wipe the information from the systems.

At the top of the building, they looked out over the vista, large glass windows allowing for an unobscured view. In fact, if not for the building itself, he might have thought himself staying in a five-star hotel. The only thing that concerned him was they hadn't yet found Colvert's hidey-hole.

Once more he pressed the communicator and waited. This time Jonah's visage appeared, exhausted. "What's wrong?" Franklin asked.

"Nothing," Jonah hedged, but Franklin had fought alongside the man for too long to be put off by his friend.

"Something's bothering you. Another attack?"

Jonah sighed heavily and shook his head. "No, but I've just received intelligence that someone is aware of your location. I'm not sure how much longer you've got. Have you found any information on the comps?"

Franklin gritted his teeth together. "No. We've collected all the main systems and thought it better to let Maylin have at them."

Jonah appeared to relax, and Franklin's internal alarm began to blare loudly. "Why? What's going on?"

"Don't turn them on. What I do need, however, is for you to find Colvert's private office. We didn't when we went through the building. We didn't have the time or the resources back then, but I think we'll find a key there. Something to help us tie up who's in charge, how to find them, and a whole heap more."

Franklin frowned. "Like what?"

Jonah shook his head. "Not now, Franklin. Once you're back on base, we'll get the team together and I'll explain it all. Just get Senna to move fast, find Colvert's office, and bring me those machines."

It sounded so simple when Jonah put it like that, but thus far, they hadn't found anything to show them where to find the office space Jonah needed them to check.

Franklin disconnected and turned to his team. "We have to find that office. Fan out. Check every level, every door and cupboard. Colvert had to have a private space, and that's what we're looking for."

They moved down the building, opening every door in a methodical fashion. The only room they ignored was the lab.

At the bottom of the building, Franklin was ready to explode.

"There's nothing here, Franklin," Sevres told him.

"There's only one room left. Let me go in first and talk to Senna." He entered the room to find her rubbing her eyes.

He checked the chrono on his wrist and swore when he saw the 0300. "Dammit. We need rest, Senna, take some time, you'll work better fresh. The men and I will take shifts watching for signs anyone knows we're here."

"I thought I almost had it." She sighed. "But when I checked—" Her shrug appeared limp.

Unable to help himself, he moved forward, curling an arm

around her waist and urging her down off the stool. Her eyelids drooped, and he cursed himself for his inattention.

"We take a break. Resume at 0800, which will give you time to rest, shower, and eat before starting again."

Her dark hair escaped from the vicious ponytail she'd pulled it back into. "No, Franklin. I know the answer is there, just out of reach, but—"

"Rest first, Senna. Otherwise, you could make a mistake. One that's fatal to hundreds."

She snapped back at his words, lips thinning and spine turning ramrod straight, then she sagged, all the fight leaving her body. "Yes, you're right. Where can I..."

He indicated a consulting room. It wasn't a great place to sleep, as he thought back to what he'd last seen here, but they'd be able to get some horizontal rest. At least there were the beds the men had shoved into two of the rooms. His body ached, particularly his ribs, and he really needed to lie down.

Even as the thought melted away, Senna leaned in and he hissed.

She reared away. "You've done too much. Dammit. Where were you anyway?"

He grimaced as her hand brushed against his side. "Searching. Looking for comps and Colvert's office."

"Colvert?"

"The guy behind the experimentation and the production cloning and tech implantation of the warrior kids."

She rubbed hands over her eyes, and his emotions roiled. "It's really a little too much to take in tonight. Where are we sleeping?"

His sigh echoed in the room. "In some consulting rooms. We grabbed therapy beds and wheeled them in, so at least we'd have something to lie on. There are enough beds to rotate the team." He ushered her into the first room, where he'd stay with her, since the team had planned on him not taking a duty tonight. "By the way, I have news—"

Senna shook her head, stopping his words. "I'm too tired. Tell me in the morning," she said and crawled onto the nearest gurney before closing her eyes. "Blessed sleep."

It irked the way she'd brushed off what he was about to say, but honestly, his mind questioned whether it would make any difference tonight or tomorrow morning. So, on that thought, he followed suit, shucking only his jacket, which he placed over the dusty pillow, and settling down. The wash of relief from the pain was immediate, and he lay still for long moments, focused on the sound of Senna's breathing until he too closed his eyes.

⁂

Franklin slept as Senna clambered off the gurney. Overnight, her mind had contemplated and spun ideas. She'd woken with a plan after allowing her mind to consider how she might successfully complete the task.

Turning, her gaze dropped to Franklin, and for just a moment, she let the situation with him cloud her mind.

She was definitely intrigued by him, but he'd brushed her off once, and she was the kind of girl that believed once was more than enough. Strangely, though, it hadn't killed her attraction to him. *Why is that?*

Shaking her head, she turned quietly and wandered into the corridor. Stomach gurgling, she wondered what arrangement they'd made for food, before the ever-present need to return to her research rose up. If only she had someone to call on, to check in with her plan. But everyone she knew who'd have some kind of understanding either had no interest in becoming involved or had gone into hiding since the battles had begun.

Senna stepped back into the lab and surveyed the room, not just the equipment as she'd done yesterday. Her mind was still playing over the idea she was incubating, so what better time to investigate? And maybe she'd find things that could be taken to the infirmary.

The door to the lab opened wide. "Everything okay in here?" questioned one of the guards she didn't know.

"Yeah, I'm just working on something."

As the door swung shut, she headed to the corner to check out a cupboard door. Bottles of chemicals, some she was sure would be welcome, remained in the temperature-controlled storage container. For the first time she mused, *I wonder where the power's coming from?*" Clearly, it had remained on during all this time without being interrupted. At each cupboard, she scanned the labels and made a mental note of the contents.

At the southeastern corner of the room, Senna discovered a door hidden by overflowing shelves, and she frowned. "I wonder where this leads to?" Pushing the barrier aside, she glanced beyond. With a deep breath. she stepped inside to examine the area. "I think I'll have to close the door and hide the light to see here." With that, she pushed.

The door opened with a groan, and Senna slid the shelves in front to the side with care then propped it open with a large box, not wishing to get caught in whatever lay beyond.

A set of illuminated steps led down to an office area. The room was comfortable with seating zones, a mini-cooler full of drinks still, and some science experiments that might once have been food, sitting on plates. "I wonder if this was his office."

Files littered the desk, and turning, she noted large tubes. She crept closer then reared back as she saw what was inside.

"Oh my God!" Skeletons, some in various stages of bio-cybernetic enhancement. "I need to show Franklin," she breathed, even as she carefully scooped up the paper files.

The computer on the desk blinked, and the urgency to look clawed at her. *What will I find?*

She reached out to touch a key then tugged her hand back, as if it burned. What if it was booby-trapped and she lost the information?

Find Franklin, echoed in her brain. She headed for the stairs as she heard the shouts.

Waking felt good. The aches in Franklin's body had subsided, though he had to adjust the regen device strapped to his chest, but when he swung his legs over the side of the gurney—and it took a moment to remember why he was on one—he was pretty pleased.

Checking his chrono, he noted the time wasn't yet 0800.

"Hey, Senna..." He turned to the gurney she'd inhabited and frowned when he realized she wasn't there.

The bed itself was rumpled, but there was no sign of a struggle, and he was a light enough sleeper that he would have heard anything untoward.

After a quick trip into the bathroom he entered the hall. Young Jennerton, a second year recruit, loitered. "Have you seen Senna?" Franklin asked.

The man-boy indicated to the lab. "Went in there about thirty minutes ago. I checked and she said she was doing something. Not sure where she's gone. I went up to the supplies to grab an MRE, and when I came back, she'd left."

Franklin frowned. "Left?"

"Thought maybe a bathroom visit, but you know. Now I don't know where she is. Gunnar and Phil are checking the levels and told me to wait here. We'd just swapped shifts about two hours ago, so the others are sleeping. Gunnar said if we don't find her, we should wake them."

Franklin rubbed his hands through his hair. Disappeared. *Where? How?*

The rate of his heartbeat increased, but maybe there was a logical explanation. Still, he had to ask, "And she hasn't come back out here?"

"Not that we saw."

He pushed open the doors to the lab. It was empty. Where was she? He scanned the room as voices echoed down the hallway. "Not here! But we've got company on the way!"

The doors swung open, and the team hurried inside, even those who were supposed to be resting, rubbing their eyes.

"What the hell is going on?" He spun and watched as a shelving unit moved, and he lurched forward as Senna hurried from behind it. "What? Where were you?"

"There's an office down there, but what's all the shouting?" She moved closer, clutching some paper files to her chest.

He sputtered and scratched the back of his neck with the ring he wore on his right hand, his mind whirling madly. He might not be the ideas guy, but he was the senior here on this mission. *What to do?*

Fzzt. Fzzt. In his pocket, an insistent buzz began. For a moment, he ignored it. Then understanding welled. "Shit!"

Eyes turned to him.

"What?" Senna demanded.

"We have incoming unfriendlies. On their way." He whirled, and she reached out, clamping her hands on his.

"How do you know we have incoming, and how long do we have?" Her voice was low, deep, and shaking with panic.

He dragged the unit from his pocket. Scanned it. The information was minimal. He'd need to know more before he could make informed decisions.

"Long-range scanner. I placed some secura-tags around the perimeter yesterday. All I know is three have entered the grounds, though two have retreated. One is still inside the grounds somewhere." His fingers tapped the screen, then he pushed, slid, and glared at the unit in his hands. "Dammit! I can't get a visual tag. But an eye-in-the-sky shows what looks like a platoon heading in this direction. We have maybe an hour—if that."

She hissed. "But I still have to—"

"No more time, Senna. Load up your equipment and anything you consider necessary. We're going to have to take this back to base now. Get everything together. We won't be back."

"But I'm at a critical phase—"

"Critical or not, our safety is key. Jennerton will carry whatever you need. Take two others and load up as much as you can, then show me this office." His mind whirled as he considered. "No! Show me now. I'll see what's there and grab what I can."

He pushed the shelving unit aside and the large box, but not before he noted the way she rolled her eyes.

"I put it there so the door wouldn't shut on me. You know, being trapped down there is not what I'd like. Especially when you get a look at what I've found." She sounded winded, but not alarmed.

Her tone intrigued him, and he trotted down after her into the lush work area.

At the bottom of the steps, Senna stilled him. "I checked the cooler, but there's nothing of value in there. The comp is over here along with some paper files. I planned to take them with me and ask about the comp."

He grunted, scanned the room, and considered how quickly he could empty the things they'd need. "Good work, Senna. We'll take it back for Maylin. See what she can find."

She turned, so her chest nestled against his. It felt really good, but it wasn't the time or place. Before he could speak though, she did. "Umm, then there's that." She pointed over his shoulder and he turned.

"Oh..." A skeleton in a tube, metallic inserts capturing his gaze. His stomach lurched. "We should..." He gulped, sickened to realize exactly what he was seeing. "We need to snap pics for Jonah."

"That's not the only one, Franklin. Behind it there's more. Children in varied states of gestation. It's...it's sickening. Horrific really."

He peered close. Bile burned its way up his throat, scouring him from the interior. "I... You take the pics. I'll grab the files." He shoved his communicator at her. "Just don't send them. We'll report this face-to-face."

War and death on a battlefield he could handle, but the vision before him was too much like a horror vid. A graphic reminder of the inhumanity he was fighting against. He turned away, needing to focus on something else while he wrestled his gut back under control. As it was, a cold sweat broke out all over his body, beading his upper lip, and the ever-present sick taste on his tongue was enough to warn him of the danger. He shivered as a chill snaked down his back.

Franklin tugged one drawer out, used it as a file box, and dumped everything into it he could find. Small backup devices he dumped into the box too, then set to dismantling the comp. Satisfied he'd found everything he needed, he ushered Senna up the stairs, handed the box to Jennerton, then proceeded to box up everything she requested. As he worked, she started opening cupboards.

"What are you doing?" he demanded.

"There's medications and things that Michael may need. Plus, I want to grab some of the equipment—"

"We don't have time, Senna. Just what's necessary."

In the end, she packed several boxes of bottles and packets as well as surgical equipment, and they loaded it into the vehicle.

Jennerton came running up, a small device in his hands. "Time's running out, sir. The eye has them almost at the grounds. We have to go."

Franklin nodded. Their safety was top priority. But he had one last task to achieve. Something he'd had the men put in place as they retrieved what they needed. "Into the vehicles and strap down. Then move forward, but keep enough room for us in the center. We've got all the files and Sergeant Reed here."

Senna climbed into his vehicle, the back obscured by boxes, but he felt the weight of her gaze as he pushed a box onto the wall. The corresponding one in his pocket.

"What are you doing?" she asked, her voice suspicious as she watched his movements.

"Making sure this location is no good to them." He started the engine, rolled it forward into the middle of the convoy as they'd agreed. At the edge of the clearing, he stopped, dipped his hand into his pocket, and drew out the tiny device. He pressed the button, and as she gasped he floored the accelerator.

"*What did you do, Franklin?*" She clutched the door and stared in horror as fire pulsed and the building rippled.

"Whatever's left, they won't be able to use." He felt no satisfaction though. It was a loss. One he was sure Jonah would agree with once they'd explained what was coming. Still, even though they couldn't afford for the equipment to fall into the warrior kids' hands, it was a loss they could ill afford.

Just before the entrance, he and the team turned their vehicles, so they traveled down a side track, then pulled up to wait.

"What have we stopped for?" Senna demanded.

"*Shhh*." Franklin placed a finger against his lips, the vehicles now hidden in the middle of the underbrush.

The ground shuddered as several aircraft zoomed overhead.

"What was that?"

"A pre-emptive strike."

"Pre-emptive...you *bombed* them?" Her eyes were wide, and he read the horror on her face.

"They would have killed us, Senna."

"But if we had that capacity, why haven't we used it before? We could have..."

"Senna, stop. *Think*. Usually they engage in an urban environment. Whoever is running their missions uses that fact to make it obvious its war against children. That's what they want the civvies to see. Except they aren't children. They're warriors. Genetically manipulated to kill. With cybe implantations that make them stronger and faster." Her face paled at the horror he was describing, but he needed her to fully understand. "Trained to slaughter us."

He understood her fears. Knew that on every front it was an untenable situation.

"You're a soldier. Were a soldier. You need to think like one again, not a civilian. It's us or them, Senna."

Her eyes closed, and a tear trickled down her cheek as she nodded slowly. "I know. I do. It's just—"

"It's yet another reason they're so efficient. It attacks every aspect of our soul and they trade on that. But we have to think of the big picture. The millions who'll pay if we don't do our job and hold the line."

She sniffed and opened her eyes. "You say you're no strategist, but that's the most strategic thinking ever. Franklin, I—"

She reached out, and it took everything in him to shake his head. "Later, Senna. Later."

CHAPTER 8

Senna and Franklin drove in the entrance to the base, followed by three additional vehicles, all of them jam-packed with comps, documents, and equipment. Franklin pulled up outside the commandant's office, and the others pulled up nearby, windows slid down.

"Take the comps to Maylin," Franklin instructed. "The lab equipment goes to the infirmary, along with the records and drugs Senna collected. Then take some downtime. Report to your officers at 1300 hours. And good work."

As they drove off, Franklin reflected on the situation at hand. One full platoon of warrior kids defeated. It had been harrowing heading back past the smoking remains, but they'd had no other option. His mind wanted to shy away from what they'd seen, but he couldn't change what they'd witnessed.

Senna followed him into the building, still gripping the communicator with all the images, both of the carnage that remained of the children and the skeletal remains found in Colvert's office.

At the door, she stopped him, her hand on his shoulder. "We're doing the right thing, I know that, but it still feels wrong. I know we have to beat them, but killing kids, no matter the situation, doesn't feel right."

Now he turned, faced her, and cupped her cheek. "I understand, and yes, it feels like the greatest betrayal, and yet it's the only way to assure humanity has a future. Come on, he'll be waiting for us."

He understood the psychological morass she was trying to overcome. Hell, he faced it too. After this was done, though, it felt as if he too would be looking to retreat away from the memories of the things they'd had to do in order to survive.

Just like those David and Erin had addressed before them. Daniella and Jonah, Michael and Clarissa too.

Perhaps, he might even discuss that with them once this war was done? *If it's ever done.* He shook away the thoughts, because for now, the focus had to be on overcoming their enemies and winning. Healing would have to wait.

The building was a seething mass of bodies. News outlets, who'd previously stayed away from the base, swarmed, and military personnel rushed to complete their reporting or to prepare mission briefs. Franklin slid an arm around Senna, and they shoved forward until they reached where Daniella and Jonah stood before a lectern, addressing the people via a vid-feed.

"The combatants were neutralized, but not without personal cost to my people," Jonah stated. "They had followed them to one of Jeremy Colvert's private facilities. He was the mastermind behind the biocybernetics implantation of the warrior children. Information is still sketchy on how many, but somewhere in the order of fifty combatants converged on my people."

Jonah eyed them down, and Franklin wondered where this newfound confidence his friend exuded had come from. Was it because of Daniella or had it been dormant the whole time, ready to emerge when needed?

His introspection was cut short by a question from the man beside him. "Is there any truth to the rumors that the colony ship will be ready in the next few days?"

Daniella strode forth and cleared her throat. "We are not in a position to comment on that, however, I will say the safety and security of our colonists is at the forefront of our minds. Now, if that's all?"

She glared, at her haughty best, her blonde hair glowing in the artificial light, makeup impeccable along with her figure-hugging white suit and her spine stiffer than a rod. "Thank you for your attendance. Media kits will be circulated on the transport back. Our people will escort you to your transports."

Senna and Franklin stepped back, watching as the sea of people departed among mutters of 'far too sure of herself' and 'who do they think they are?'

Jonah and Daniella came forward once the door was shut. "Glad you're okay. What do you have for us?" Jonah said.

They were about to answer when the door opened and a woman rushed inside, spraying red paint at them and screaming, "Murderers! You're killing children!"

Franklin blocked Senna as Jonah shielded Daniella. Personnel streamed in, grabbing the woman and tugging her outside. Once she was gone, Daniella shivered. "They don't understand, do they? No matter what we say or how we show them, they think these warriors are children. They're not!" Her voice broke, and Franklin watched as Jonah pulled her close, whispering. Senna shivered beside him.

"Your report, Franklin," Jonah demanded.

"Worse than we thought. This is what we found." He took the communicator from Senna and showed him the images. Daniella watched on, clearly shocked, color leaching from her face.

"That's... That's horrible. Obscene!" She tottered away, then sank heavily onto a chair nearby.

"We retrieved what we could in terms of equipment and resources. The comps are on their way to Maylin and the reports to Michael. He'll be able to make sense of them—"

"Along with Windhower and the professor," interposed Daniella, who'd visibly pulled herself together. The attack had really shaken her, Franklin realized having never seen that before.

"Yes. But the files are sensitive. I'd hate for Clarissa to see them." Franklin stared at Jonah who shrugged.

"That's Michael's call, of course. But it may give us an indication of what we don't know. We have the records of the fertility clinics, and that was damning enough. When it comes to working out the numbers of enemy combatants and their approximate ages, this will be a huge bonus. At least we'll have a better idea of the ones Colvert was involved in. At this point we don't know how many more clinics and combatants from other continents exist. We're waiting on the intel, but it's hard to gain accurate information."

Franklin harrumphed, more than aware that it was what they didn't know that posed danger.

Senna thrust up a hand before asking, "Did we ever work out their designations?"

Jonah winced. "Yes. We did. According to what we've been able to work out, each of the letters in their name corresponds to the 'donor' parent."

"So Liv—"

"LV-1, which is a derivative of the parents and their sequential number of cloning."

"Oh my God!" Senna's eyes grew round. "You mean there is more than one LV?"

Franklin shook his head, clearly lost. "We really don't know how many there are. It's why these files are so important. It should, or could, give us a clue. And heaven knows, we need as much information as we can lay our hands on."

"Okay then, Senna and Franklin, you did great. Get the last of the information over to Michael. We'll call a full senior briefing at 1400 hours to sift through what we've gleaned. By then we should have an idea from Maylin on what she can access from the comps," Jonah said then turned away to concentrate on another task.

Dismissed, both Senna and Franklin headed back outside into the sunlight. Senna shook as if removing the last vestiges of cold from her system. "There's so much we don't know. Tell me, Franklin, do you think we can win this?" She pinned him with her gaze.

He glanced at her, wondering how she could possibly echo his thoughts so perfectly. "I have no idea. I'd like to think we can, but there's still a long way to go, Senna. A long way."

CHAPTER 9

After they'd dropped off the files, Franklin left Senna at the building she had been billeted in. Before she got out of the vehicle, she turned back to the man sitting in the driver's seat. "I was really hard on you over the last couple of days, and particularly the other night. I took your rebuttal wrong, and I apologize. You're a good man, Franklin, and you sell yourself short."

She didn't stop the gentle caress of her hand over his cheek. Her psyche screamed to keep it gentle and light, but even in the vehicle, the innate intimacy of the action left her nerves dancing with excitement and perhaps a dash of hope.

"I'll see you later," she said.

She slid out of the car before he could say anything else, aware that she'd pushed the limits of their connection to its maximum, at least for now. In her mind, it was akin to a dance. One step to the side, two steps forward, then a quick retreat before starting again.

After shutting the car door, she turned to the building, a gray and anonymous slab of block, and sighed. *Isn't this a luxurious retreat?* She almost snorted at the whimsy. She tugged her bag over her shoulder and felt it settle in place. Moving quickly, Senna reached the external stairs as a hand landed on her shoulder. She whirled, amazed to see that it was Franklin.

"Senna, I was the one who said the wrong thing in the wrong way. You didn't do anything to apologize for." The turmoil in his eyes stole her breath.

"I—"

He shook his head. "You were right when you said I was hiding from the truth. I was. I haven't been overly successful with women, because I was always afraid I'd turn out like my old man. I never shared myself fully with them, because he was abusive. Hit my mother at any given opportunity, and I distrusted myself because of that experience. My mother passed when I was thirteen after some random accident, and after that, he brought a succession of women into the household. Treated them all the same way as far as I saw until I got away on my sixteenth birthday. Joined the corps and dedicated myself to it."

Her heart lurched. He was sharing the most negative, and probably intimate, aspect of his history with her, baring his soul. It also explained why he'd shied away, and she felt dirty. Low. As if she'd reinforced the negativity that he'd lived in during his formative years.

"You're not like him, Franklin. You're a caring man. Protective and honest."

He turned away, and she wanted to sigh but held back the sound. *He deserves better.*

"I'm just me, Senna. I'm not a hero, or someone wearing a cape who's going to save the world. Just a guy."

"You're more than just any guy. Thank you for sharing that with me." She leaned in and kissed him softly on the lips as sparks of invisible electricity arced between them.

His eyes widened, and she pulled back, not wanting to frighten him away. Desperate to hold onto any ground she gained.

Franklin shrugged and glanced away. "I just wanted you to know why I..." He breathed deeply, his chest rising and falling hard.

"Thank you for trusting me with your past. I won't betray your trust."

His short nod told her he'd given her a gift, even if he didn't yet realize it. Then he turned and strode away.

Franklin didn't know why he'd shared that information, just that he had. Now, as he sat in the briefing room, his awareness of Senna, sitting across the aisle from him, bloomed. He wasn't so much confused as puzzled by the need to explain himself. It wasn't his usual way of doing things, and certainly not the kind of information he'd ever shared with a woman. Before another thought could occur, he ended it.

He grunted, concentrating on those present as more people crowded in. Michael was there, but Clarissa was noticeably absent as he slumped into the seat beside Franklin.

"Where's Clarissa?"

"At the rooms with Eliza. She's upset after I told her about the files you found. I scanned them, Franklin. The things that bastard Colvert did..."

"Like what?"

Michael's hand fisted as his face took on a vicious slant. "I swear, I could kill him right now." His voice vibrated with fury, and Franklin turned, noting the white bracketing his friend's mouth. Michael shook his head, eyes glinting. "He's a monster. I reported it all to Jonah and Daniella, and they're horrified. He used her as a lab rat." His friend inhaled deeply, nostrils flaring.

"Anything I can do?"

Michael shook his head. "No."

Dismissed, Franklin focused on the front as Jonah entered the room, his face thunderous, brows drawn tight, and cheeks ruddy with anger. "Listen up! We've got lots to discuss, and time's running tight."

Those gathered in the room who hadn't yet sat down took their seats, the hubbub of chatter dying away.

"We've been informed all checks on the colony ship will take place over the next forty-eight hours. You're all here because you're either a specialist we need or you've been involved in the implementation of the security forces or the public relations arm of our campaign. We've also received intel that points to a massed attack happening in the next seventy-two hours, prior to the colonists arriving for the boarding of the first ship. We can't allow that."

Maylin hurried to the podium set up at the front of the room. "I've been monitoring the secure channels for the last couple of weeks, and while I can't be certain that they aren't baiting us, we know they want control of the ships. We also know they've managed to lay their hands on ground-to-air missiles. If that's the case, which is what's been indicated in communications, then they can attack the ship at any point, even after they deploy."

The lump Franklin was trying to avoid acknowledging grew larger in his gut. They had to get the first ship off safely. Anything else was horrific to consider.

Daniella stepped up as Maylin moved away. "We have also come into possession of a large body of evidence concerning the warrior children program. We know it's been accepted by the Illegan Government, however, it is beyond their powers to entertain and participate in this level of genetic manipulation. This means the 21st Testing Protocol is *ultra vires*." She gripped the wood lectern and gazed at those listening, as if she willed them to absorb her words into their bodies.

People muttered, asking what those words meant.

"They have *no legal capacity to enact this law*." She stopped, gathered her breath, and composed herself. "Per statute 53. 'In order for a protocol to become enacted in law, no move can have been made to institute such actions in premeditation.' They have broken faith with the populace, and we've taken a hit since the release of the footage showing the attacks on these children."

Mutters grew louder as she made eye contact with everyone gathered in the room.

"At this point, they're ahead of us in the PR game. The public's trust in us has been severely dented as a result. It's time for us to take back that control. We must set the record straight and regain our true government. I won't lie and say it's going to be easy or swift." Daniella paused, waited, but the room was silent enough that even the shuffle of a foot would be audible. "Even if we win the war, there will be pockets of unrest, but this new information is damning. It shows their insidious plans have been in train for years. They planned these abominations. They never meant to help our society, only to strip control and take it for themselves."

The stark white of her skin and the glow of her hair shined under the lights, and not for the first time, Franklin was struck by how she captured the attention of all with not just her words, but also her appearance. Here was no meek and mild woman, but a tigress intent on reaffirming the laws of their world.

Applause broke out, some standing in ovation, and she waited for those assembled to retake their seats. "Jonah has also received intelligence about the children who were taken from the facility. At an appropriate time, the adoptive parents will be given access to this information as well as our resident medical personnel. I, personally, would like to thank each and every one of you. Those under your leadership. To everyone who has pledged themselves to this effort. Thank you." Then Daniella walked away from the podium and waited by the door.

Jonah stepped forward once more. "One last piece of intelligence has come to light from the other continents. Most of the northern hemisphere continents are in the grips of similar battles. The locations of the other colony ships which are under construction in other countries have been kept covert, yet it seems the warrior children have become aware of them. We don't know if the information was leaked or if they simply stumbled onto them. It has been agreed by each continent commander that we focus on this location initially, particularly aware that this will be the first launch location."

His face tense, Jonah took a breath, then continued.

"*When* we overcome the children—and make no mistake, we will —we'll send reinforcements and intel to assist with the battle everywhere else. This is truly a worldwide phenomenon, people. We must win, because anything else potentially will lead to genocide of our race. *That cannot happen.* Assignments will be handed to you at the door. Read them. Digest the information, then return your written orders to us. No documentation is to leave this room. All information being disseminated is purely need-to-know, and we can't afford leaks at this crucial point. Good luck everyone, and may the gods be on our side. Dismissed."

CHAPTER 10

*S*enna tapped her fingers on the device she'd finally managed to finish satisfactorily. The last twenty-four hours had passed in a blur as she'd requested Professor Venos's assistance. In the end, it was simple enough to add a single chemical to combine the elements and create the filter they required. It rankled even though she felt immense satisfaction at the knowledge that her work would be integral in the safety of the colonists.

Glancing at the framed image on the wall by a window, the newly renamed *President Yin* would be an Alpha Class Colony Ship with the designation of 001 in honor of the murdered president. It would be imposing on the horizon, no doubt, once the silo-like building housing it peeled away.

She turned away. "I'll be able to see it from this window," she murmured, having glanced out, seeking the dimming light of the glorious sunset which framed the silver and white structure on the horizon. Twilight turned the sky azure with a hazy overlay of ochre and crimson.

The door to the office space she'd been allocated while she planned and carried out the mission opened, and Franklin stepped within. She slid the seat around and turned in the direction of the sound that heralded his arrival.

Not for the first time, she physically felt his proximity.

Franklin speared his blunt fingers through his hair. "I've got our people organized as you requested. The scanners are stashed in the vehicle for tomorrow morning, and they'll report onsite at 0600, ready to begin the inspection."

Her stomach jittered. "It's surreal, knowing that tomorrow we'll be walking through the colony ship. Making it safe for the hundreds going first."

He dropped into the seat opposite her, the desk looming between them. "So, why didn't you put your hand up?"

Cocking her head, Senna stared at him. "For what?"

"The colony ship. You could have gone and likely would have had a better than even chance to be picked for any of the next couple."

She steepled her fingers on the desk and considered the question. "I honestly don't know," she hedged. "Maybe I thought I still had something to give to our planet, or maybe I didn't think I had a chance. There's a lot who didn't apply, and any one of a million reasons why."

But it wasn't the only reason. *Should I tell him what was happening? Will he think less of me when he knows?* The uncustomary reticence sat poorly, but sharing something so important to her wasn't easy.

"Why didn't you, Franklin?" The question took him by surprise given the way he sputtered.

"I'm still a member of the corps so unable to apply. Rules are rules." His gaze moved over her shoulder to the view through the window.

"But you're working with, and you are part of, a senatorial investigation group. Doesn't that trump your corps association?" Wrinkling her brow, she wondered how that had actually come about.

He sighed and looked back to her, his gaze piercing in intensity. "Now, that's a story and a half. After Clarissa was found and we became aware of Colvert's work, the team was created by Daniella at Yin's direction. Then we had the coup that overthrew the government and Yin was murdered. Once Daniella was implicated, there was no going back, and we had to spirit her away before the children attacked. Even though the corps is committed to the cause of returning the government, I'd thrown my lot in with Jonah, Michael, David, and Daniella. No political associations, even of a personal level, are allowed, so I would have struck out. But by then, they'd already made the selection for the first five ships, so it was too late anyway."

Senna inhaled, taking the plunge. "I wanted to apply. When it came time to get the references though, that's when the mess with my investigations turned up, and my senior officer refused to sign the paperwork. I could have spoken to Michael as a previous supervisor, but it was straight after his accident. Strangely, it's also the time I started seeing traces of the compound." And now that she'd met Franklin, her will to consider it further withered like a leaf on a vine in the middle of a scorching summer day. "Maybe sometime in the future."

His gaze met hers, the frisson of awareness sparking around them. "Perhaps." His voice deepened, and in the pit of her belly, the swelling need boiled.

"Franklin, I—"

"Senna—"

They laughed, a little of the pressure evaporating from the room for just a moment, as they considered how they must sound. Then that small bit of whimsy disappeared.

"Senna, I was wrong about you. I do want to explore what's between us. I just..." He shrugged as if this conversation were an everyday occurrence, but she read his discomfort in his eyes.

She smiled. "So do I. We could start again?"

His laugh filled the void that she hadn't realized yawed deep inside. "You're willing to give it a shot after my reaction?"

She pushed out of the chair and rounded the desk, aware that he'd stood up to meet her. When Senna reached him, she hesitated, unsure what to do next as she rubbed her thumbs against her pant legs.

He reached out, palms upward, and her heart skipped a beat or several. Nervously, she slid her fingers over his palms. His latched on and tugged her closer. "Senna, please." It wasn't a plea but a siren's call, and she leaned in, hoping for a kiss.

Her eyes drooped to half-mast, then closed completely when their lips met. The touch was gentle, like the beat of a butterfly's wings. His breath whispered along the seam of her mouth, and she opened to him.

Her body vibrated with the sudden roar of hunger. It arced through her nervous system, jumping from point to point. Tiny dots of fireworks erupting in her psyche until he pulled away.

The drugging essence of their connection faded, and she opened her eyes, noting the grin on his face.

"That was—" She groped for the best word to describe how she felt, and gasped, "amazing," then winced at the banality.

"So, what now?" Franklin asked as he enfolded her in a hug, and she crowded closer, listening to the beat of his heart, now in tune with her own.

"Slow," she whispered against the steely hardness of his chest. "There's too much happening for the rush right now."

Senna felt Franklin's sigh of dissatisfaction. That reassured her as nothing else could.

Her stomach rumbled. "Dinner I think. But let's try somewhere else, okay? The mess hall sucks."

He guffawed at her announcement. "Your wish is my command, lady."

They pulled away from each other, and she felt the instant loss of his touch all the way to her gut.

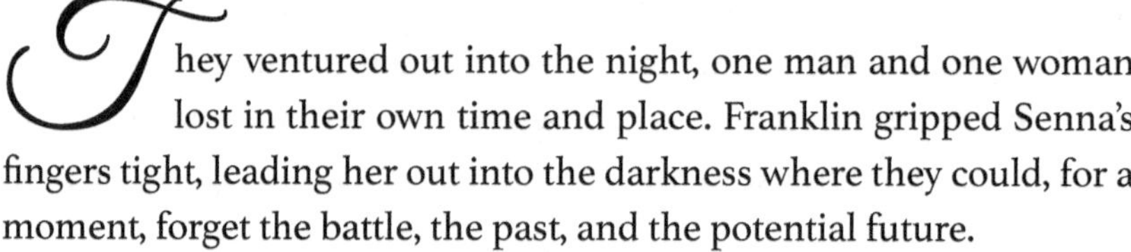

They ventured out into the night, one man and one woman lost in their own time and place. Franklin gripped Senna's fingers tight, leading her out into the darkness where they could, for a moment, forget the battle, the past, and the potential future.

He wanted more than dinner right now, the primal hunger simmering beneath the surface, but that was what they'd agreed to.

He'd be damned if he'd stuff this opportunity up with impatience. Besides, they'd need to be up early in the morning, in time for the 0600 start at the silo.

He urged her forward, toward Clarissa and Michael's home.

"Clarissa is cooking, so we'll join them, then we can take some time, have a drink with our friends, and go into the night. *Just us.*"

Her tension was palpable, fingers pushing down hard on his. "Is that okay with them?"

"We have a standing invitation, Senna."

She nodded, a stiff acknowledgement, but he read the nerves in the way she jerked her head up and down. "Okay."

At the door, he turned and pulled her against him. Kissed her with a light touch then released her. He wanted her to latch on and take more, but this wasn't the time or the place. *Which sucks!*

She cleared her throat. "Umm, what was that for?"

"To keep you going through the meal."

Now Senna laughed—a tinkle that rode across his nerve endings like a gentle caress.

As a couple, they entered the room, and Franklin was aware of the speculative glances that shot their way. He waited for a comment or query, but they remained silent. *Not sure if this is good or not.*

The meal was yet another simple and basic stew, but tasty and a great improvement from the variety of slush served in the mess. Once the meal was done, the clearing attended to, and the goodbyes offered, they rose and thanked Clarissa and Michael for their hospitality.

Senna exited first, but before Franklin could follow, Michael clasped him on the shoulder. "You've chosen well, my friend."

Unable to form a reply, Franklin simply nodded then joined Senna on the stoop.

"Ready?" she asked.

The breathless quality of her voice melted him. He wondered if it was because she was a strong woman or the arousal that curled around the two of them. *Probably a mix of both.*

"Let's go," he replied.

They strode into the night, two people looking for time together. Alone.

Making their way to the gardens at the end of the parade ground, he pulled her down onto the seat beside him. "How are we traveling?"

"On foot?" she quipped back, and he laughed.

He wasn't a man given to long speeches or second-guessing his actions, yet this tentative romance was beyond his experience. "No, I mean the situation between us. I want more, Senna, but I understand the need to take our time."

Senna nestled in. "I haven't had a lot of relationships, but this feels right." Her head settled on his shoulder, and he felt the whisper of her breath on his neck. "It's new, and we haven't had a lot of time, but I think we're doing okay."

Franklin's chest expanded as a sense of peace filled him at her words. He wanted and needed this to work. He'd expected to never experience this sense of rightness or belonging, and yet, here he was, with Senna.

"When I was a little boy, my mother would tell me that one day a princess would come along and I'd know." A lump formed in his throat, the memory hazy, but in his mind, the voice of his mother echoed. "She said I'd know when she turned up, and I would do the right thing by her." The cold that clutched his guts at the memory of his mother melted away. "I think you're the princess I was supposed to seek out."

Her fingers clutched at his sleeve. "I thought we were supposed to take this slow, Franklin. I can't..." She moved, sitting up and creating a separation between them. The eyes she turned in his direction shined with tears. "I can't say with any certainty that I'm your princess. I can tell you I'd like to be, but more than that..." She shrugged, and he understood.

"You need time, and so do I. I just wanted to tell you that." Cupping her chin with his hand, he propelled her forward so their lips met. The kiss was gentle, yet it fanned the flames of desire.

Passion rolled like a wave over both of them as the kiss deepened. Lips and tongues moved as one while he gripped her shoulders so they remained close despite the gap between their bodies. When Franklin and Senna drew away, their breathing was frantic, chests moving quickly as their heaving lungs sucked in the oxygen they both needed.

"I want more, Senna. But not tonight. Tonight we forge what is between us. Tomorrow we do the job, but once that's done..."

She nodded. "I know."

Without the further need for words, they rose in concert and walked back to the lines, hands entwined and heading back to their lonely accommodation.

orning came far too early for Senna's liking. The dream had been subtly erotic, with herself and Franklin on a beach somewhere, and things were getting interesting as the blare of her alarm started. Senna opened her eyes on a groan, reached over, and smacked the electronic alarm with a thud.

0500. *Great.* She crawled out of the bed on a sigh. "Some days are easier than others," she groused, reaching for her uniform.

Once clothed, she stomped to the bathroom, her bootsteps only partially muffled by the carpeting, and groomed herself. Finally comfortable with her appearance, she turned for the door. It opened beneath her touch, and she stepped out into the hall and smacked into a wide chest. One she'd seen naked in her dreams.

"Oh, Franklin," she murmured as the urge to reach up and kiss him rose.

"I brought breakfast." In his hands were two packets, and she wondered what they might be. "Let's head on over early. You can run through the process again and we can eat before anyone else arrives."

Now there's a plan I can get behind. They trotted down the steps, Senna's room being on the third floor, and while it remained dark they heard and saw movement under the false lighting.

He reached out and directed her to the vehicle about twenty steps away from the bottom of the stairs.

Franklin dropped the bags in her lap once they'd climbed in, and he started the engine. "Today's going to be frantic with the crew going over the ship. I thought this way at least we could have some quiet time before the madness." A crimson tinge spread over his cheeks, delighting Senna.

"I'm amazed that you've always decried yourself as not a strategist and yet here is the proof otherwise," she teased.

"Yeah, don't make this out to be more than it is, Senna. My wanting to find quiet time alone with you before the masses descend doesn't make me a master of strategy."

Instead of arguing with him, Senna simply smiled. "Today's effort is going to be a massive step toward getting that colony ship out there. This is where we get to make a difference."

He simply grunted.

"You're not really into this whole 'one step in a major event' thing, are you?"

"It's not that I'm not interested or aware that every bit we do makes a difference, it's just that it's a small part of the whole."

Senna considered his answer. "Yet every small part is significant. If we didn't offer our skills, then they could potentially be blown up. If the engineers scrimped on their tasks—"

He rounded the corner, pulled the vehicle to a stop outside the silo, then held up his hands with a smile. "Okay, I get it."

He turned off the engine. "0532, so we don't have a lot of time." He reached over and tugged her across the console, their lips meeting. The kiss was gentle, and when they'd finished, she pulled away with a sigh.

"Now that's the way I like to be met every day." Senna tossed him one of the bags and he caught it. "Nice reflexes."

In silence they ate the nutrition muffins he'd brought, and as they finished and drank the tubes of water, the first of their crew started to arrive.

"Time for duty," she muttered and climbed from the vehicle.

Senna's crew gathered around as she reached into the boot for one of the lockboxes while Franklin tugged the larger box from the rear seat. Once they had all the containers on the ground, she flicked the locks and started handing them out.

"Remember, everyone works with a partner," she said. "You find anything, you tag myself or Franklin. This isn't the time for heroics. If these compounds are found, remember they are volatile. Do not touch the item affected. Your job is to contact us. We need to know which item, the location, and any identifying information, then clear the area."

They had secured a safe-explode box which waited on the back seat. She just hoped they didn't need it.

"All right, if you're set, go directly to your sectors. Remember, methodical and slow is acceptable. Any engineers or others who give you grief, send them my way."

Senna spied the head of the construction crew hovering in the silo and headed in his direction.

The man's gaze roamed over her body, and if the appreciative gleam in his eyes was an indicator, he liked what he saw. She didn't feel any such compunction to return the compliment, and especially not with Franklin hovering beside her, drawing her gaze.

"Major Safreed, as you see, my people have been deployed now."

"Indeed, and how long do you expect this to take? I'd like to prepare the loading process later today."

They'd already gone through this song and dance, but she'd determined he was a singular individual who wanted things his way.

"As I explained yesterday, this is a large vessel. My team must search every nook and cranny, and the devices will require recharging in the next four hours. We've managed to increase the battery charge process but—"

"I need a timeframe, sergeant."

She shrugged. "I can't give you that. If they find something, then it will take what it takes."

Safreed scowled. "Not good enough. Your commander stated we'd be good to go—"

"As soon as the job is done, major. I will not risk my people or the lives of the colonists. You're just going to have to sit tight like everyone else."

The burly man made a move, but Franklin slipped between them. "You don't want to do that, major."

The man snarled, "What do you think you're doing, *private*?"

Senna's hackles rose, but Franklin simply placed a hand on her arm. "I'm doing what I'm supposed to do. If you have further queries regarding Sergeant Reed's process, I'd suggest you direct them to either Commander McDowell or Senator Villede. And now, if you'll excuse us?"

Franklin's words dripped with ice, and Safreed backed away, hearing the jagged intent in his voice.

Franklin removed his hand from Senna's arm and indicated to the main door. "We should get started."

Senna hefted her unit, grateful they'd made loops allowing them to suspend on straps. These beasts were heavy, and she guessed they'd all have strained and sore arms by the end of the day.

Stepping inside the craft was like entering one of the laboratories. Every wall was festooned with white ceramic tiles and the metallic surfaces.

"Where to first?" Franklin asked.

She directed him to the room where rows of suspension pods lay. The colonists would enter a form of suspended animation for the longest portion of their journey. The pods would sustain them, track vital signs, and offer medical assistance should that be necessary in flight.

"We check every pod, inside and out, down to the resistance clamps and body form." Switching on her unit, she waited a moment, until the whine of the power draw settled to an eerie buzz. Senna waved her arm. "You do that side, and I'll do this one. We meet on the middle rows."

The work was laborious as they waved the wand, eyes on the monitor, looking for the ochre signal.

No one hailed them, and no ochre detected, she rubbed her aching back. "I'll be glad when we've finished this pass."

They met in the middle of the room, her monitor flashing the low battery alert, and they retreated back to the vehicle at the base of the silo.

Team members were unplugging their units, and Agent Fairburn, one of the original team, flashed a smile. "They've got the battery refill down to about thirty minutes."

She grabbed a tube of water as Franklin set their batteries to charge, then she demanded an update from everyone.

"We're all getting negative readings, Senna. If this continues, we should be able to finish this pass efficiently. Then I suppose we start on the cargo loading?"

Senna nodded and stared at the long, silver ship. Shaped like a missile, it would carry the colonists out into the universe, where they'd travel nearly four and a half light years until they landed on Agaria Minor.

"I wonder what it would be like to be the first humans on one of those M-Class planets," a woman to her left said.

"Lonely," quipped another searcher. "And with no house and only the food contained in the cargo bay until you can get the crops up. Scary to think it might fail because there isn't enough food after traveling all that distance."

"At least you wouldn't have the warrior children though," said a third searcher, and not for the first time, Senna shivered at that thought.

If they gained control of the ship, they could potentially populate the universe and wipe out other species. It was what they were already attempting to do here.

Senna didn't hurry them back to their work, aware of the muscular punishment they were all feeling right now. When the last two units were unhooked, she sent them back into the ship.

CHAPTER 11

After two days of inspection on the colony ship, Senna gave the green light to set up the loading process. Franklin was both pleased they'd detected no explosive compounds and yet concerned that it all went so well. *Something just isn't right.*

Franklin cradled a cup of hot coffee in his hands. "How do we ensure the safety of our colonists?"

Senna took a long draught of the bitter brew. "Safety isn't the only issue, Franklin." She wiggled her toes and sighed as he watched. "We have to streamline the process, otherwise we'll be doing this for the next three months."

There was a large part of the problem he noted. Too much. Too long. The colonists wanted on *now*, and Daniella did too. The responsibility he'd assumed along with Senna bit deep like a knife.

"If we talk to Maylin, perhaps we could find a way to build a larger filter," he suggested.

Senna placed her cup back on the desk, then reclined back into her seat, rubbing her eyes. "And while that's great and will work for later on, we need to break it all down now. Everything is going to have to be checked before storage in the bins for transport."

"I know, but the kickback from slowing down the operation—"

"That's Jonah's problem, Franklin. Our job is to check it and give the okay," Senna answered.

If only it were that simple. Added to that was the sense that in the darkness an attack was brewing. There'd been no incursions by the warrior children in over a week, an unusual period of silence. One that he knew couldn't last.

"They're regrouping, Franklin. I know it." Senna opened her eyes, sharing her inner turmoil with him, as if she'd read his mind.

"I agree. Once the word is out that we're bringing in the colonists, I'm certain they'll make a move. They almost have to." That ate at him all day long. The unceasing knowledge that the calm would break, and soon, and they'd likely have hundreds of civilians to protect along with the god damned ship.

"I keep thinking about this morning's briefing, Franklin. The teams are following the breadcrumbs and seeking background on Lilly Montaine as they think she's the instigator, but she's not been found. No one disappears. They can't."

He closed his eyes, considering Jonah's earlier words. "If Senator Montaine continues to stonewall... He's got quite a wall of security around his family. He's blocking the media from finding them. He's either paid them off or there's more to it."

"But this is life and death. He's a senator." Her voice carried a wealth of disgust.

"You spoke with Erin." He cocked his head to one side. "What did she have to say?"

"That once this is done, if she never sees another search string again, she'll be happy. Seriously though, she and David are working around the clock, looking for any known association. She's found bits about arms deals, but it's not enough."

"It's like we were fed the World Bank and Gantry along with the other foundations we've managed to find."

"It still doesn't tell us how we're going to find Lilly Montaine though."

"Houses and investments should be a matter of public record," sputtered Franklin, bitterness betraying the fact that they were being denied access to the very information that would save many.

Senna nodded. "I know, but Montaine didn't place them in his personal name or that of his wife. According to Erin, he created a series of lower level entities and hid them behind walls that we didn't know existed."

"I have to say, I'm pleased we have Maylin and her team sifting through public records. It's just that doing that is tying up valuable resources." Weariness now cascaded, and he rubbed his face, wanting to clear the grittiness from his eyes. "We're no help either, tied up checking for the explosive compound, and meanwhile—" Franklin's eyes snapped open, because they all knew the truth and they all had a lot to lose now. "They're likely preparing for a full-on attack."

He turned to watch Senna shake her head. "I'm not so sure we'll get a full-on attack. Not yet. It doesn't make sense. Why expend all your energy in one burst, even if we're split three ways? Why not send a percentage of your troops? Take out what you can and damage our defenses—"

"What was that, Senna? Keep some in reserve so when we go to launch, they've got fresh resources, we won't be ready, and *boom!*" It was too horrific to accept, and yet it made sense to him. "Have you informed Jonah?"

She made a moue with her mouth. "I couldn't get near him today. I'm hoping you can get me in to see Jonah and Daniella so I can tell them what I think is going to happen." She bit her lip hard enough that blood welled, and the sight of the scarlet had him closing his eyes. *A lot of blood will be shed if this comes to pass.*

He stood up and speared her with a harsh glance. "Come on, we'll go find them."

Senna followed his lead, and at the door, he barred her exit, took her hand in his, and looked deep into her eyes. "Senna, if this is the case, I need you to promise you'll stay safe." The knowledge of what may come to pass hammered in his brain, a spike of pain blooming in his psyche.

She didn't agree. On her face he read that she'd be out there fighting, risking herself, and the knife in his gut twisted, because he knew and understood the reason for her silence. She wouldn't lie to him. He'd already grasped the fact that she was honest to a fault. By remaining quiet, she told him she'd do whatever it took, and he sighed. He couldn't blame her, because if she'd asked the same, he knew what his answer would be. That knowledge condemned his request.

"Okay, point made. At least try to stay safe."

"I will, Franklin. Can you promise the same?" Her thumb caressed the top of his hand, nearly stealing his sense.

"Yes."

*J*onah waited, his face a serious mask while Daniella clearly hadn't considered any of the news she and Franklin just shared.

"You're sure of this?"

Senna shook her head. "No, Jonah. There's no substantial intel, but look at the timeline of events. They wait until something big and visible takes place. Daniella attacked at the parliament building during the vote, then attacking her home quickly afterward. The attacks on the base just as you cleared the home and the incubation sites. The World Bank as you got close to working out who was behind it and its destruction. We know they've previously tapped into communications, so they're aware of our processes. We need a plan. Either reinforce or attack, but *something has to give*. Once we finish the scans of the cargo, you'll be bringing in the civilians. Soft targets. The teams are fractured right now, and we're vulnerable."

Jonah hissed, rubbing his eyes with a trembling hand. Michael and Clarissa, David and Erin, along with Franklin waited as she laid out her suspicions.

"We need to prepare for an attack." The desperation in her voice laid her bare.

"That's what we've been doing," interposed Daniella, but Senna shook her head.

"Yes and no. If they attempt a frontal attack, especially now, we're unprepared. Those reinforcements that were due to arrive? We need them in place today. The men here on the base haven't had real downtime in weeks, and that kind of waiting is mentally exhausting."

"Senna's right. Our people are weary. We're all looking at things from a range of directions. We need backup and we need a plan ready for this attack as just one of many. If one of those kids was able to breach our defenses, and let's be honest, during the influx of civilians that's going to be easy until we've scanned them and their items, they can create havoc. Dozens and hundreds could die, Jonah. Our defenses are already weak—"

Here Jonah smiled; a small grin to be sure, but his lips widened. "That's actually not quite true. I've had Maylin and her team work on a covert strategy for us. One that we're starting to see results with."

Senna frowned. "What?"

"The biocybernetics implants still need to be powered, right?"

Senna waited a heartbeat then shrugged. "I guess so."

Michael cleared his throat. "The warrior children have a range of implants that rely on the implantation of a small battery device at the base of their skulls. We hadn't shared that because we wanted to see if we could exploit it."

"And?"

"And we can disrupt the flow of power. It's a short-term option, but one we can utilize to our benefit. We bring them in through a powered gateway, the civilians, I mean. As they move through, a low-level charge is released. It's enough to tamper with their children's cybernetics for around fifteen minutes, during which time we scan them and their so-called carry-on items."

Franklin held up his hands, face screwed tight, and he mouthed aspects of the information Michael shared as if he wanted to speak, but he didn't say a word They waited for Jonah to continue, but he didn't.

"Let me get this right, it interrupts the implants, but even so how will you know they are targets?"

Jonah sighed. "It seems the interruption of the cybernetics will cause a range of telltale actions from shaking extremities to them passing out. It's not fatal," he hastened to add, "just incapacitating for a period of time."

"Clarissa has an inbuilt monitor, and we're fairly sure that the same exists for the other children, we just don't know how efficient it is, because once the brain is dead the attached implants fail as well, so we haven't been able to find a live test subject."

Her stomach boiled at the thought of live test subject. She knew what they'd done and how. *God help us if we start doing the same thing.*

Michael cleared his throat. "What we do know though, is if they have even a more basic version, they'll be instantly aware, meaning those who remain conscious will be ready to fight once they're able to again." The pronouncement sent a shaft of panic directly to her gut.

"Will my people be in danger? What about the civilians?" Franklin sat upright, his face tight and fists clenched.

"This is where we need a tactical crew on standby at the control site. I've already hand-picked a crew and believe we should be in a position to—"

Now Senna raised her hand, cutting Jonah off. "What about, if they are a compromised unit, Jonah? We know they're not averse to using their own as martyrs. What if they're carrying an incendiary or bomb inside them? Can we be sure this isn't the case?"

The gasps of those in the room showed very few had considered this.

"We've already worked on this possibility, Senna. The room where we scan is to be isolated, reinforced with projectile resistant plating. It's not perfect, but there's no way to make it so. We're just going to have to deal from this point on."

CHAPTER 12

Franklin eyed the lines of waiting civilians from outside the building. Senna had managed to talk them into staggering the input, citing the fact that those waiting would be a target too good to miss. Thankfully, the powers had listened to her advice.

Groups of thirty-five arrived at a time, the transports under heavy guard. Families, some with young children, trooped up to the building they'd prepared for scanning their items and the purported x-ray. Final medical scans were undertaken in the rear of the building as they made their way through the layers of procedures.

At the end of the long day, they'd put through three batches already and today's final group was almost complete. Only one man remained, as Senna's gaze met Franklin's in the scanning room. Their final target of the day was in his mid-thirties, his blond hair close cut and his eyes a watery gray.

His gait was loose, as were his clothes, as he stepped within the scanning unit. "Is this necessary?" he enquired. A hint of desperation about him tugged at Franklin's mind as he closed the door.

"It will just take a moment," Senna said as she depressed the button.

The man screamed, and Franklin hit the button for lockdown just as the man within tore at his shirt.

The whirring of locks echoed as Senna bellowed, "We've got a problem!"

Their captive charged the reinforced plasglass unit. The doors shuddered but remained firmly locked as he shoved against them.

"You bastards!" screamed the man, spittle gathering at the edges of his mouth. "You'll pay for this."

Beneath the strips of cloth, Jonah could see a device, wires and lights, and he knew. *Mother of Satan*. "He's got something, Senna!"

Senna had already seen it. "Yeah, I know," she answered and attempted to run the jamming sequence, fingers flying across the keyboard.

A shudder followed a loud *pop* as red, gray, and beige spattered the inside of the unit.

Nausea welled, and glancing at Senna, he noted the pasty gray of her complexion. Senna slumped down. "God!"

The room's doors flew open, and the tactical team ran inside, sliding to a stop. "Too late?"

Franklin nodded. There didn't seem to be the need for words.

"We'll send a clean-up team." the efficient woman in charge stated, and Franklin moved over to Senna and tugged her up into his arms.

"We'll get out of your hair then." He led her out into the twilight. It wasn't the first time either of them had seen a death, yet this one scored him from the inside.

"Why? I mean, the death was pointless. He's dead. We've got scanners now that will detect and..." Senna stopped, both feet planted as she looked at him. Tears welled in her eyes, but there was fury too. "His death was pointless. Useless. What can they gain from that?"

Franklin couldn't answer the question, so he merely shrugged.

"I'm tired of useless deaths, Franklin. There doesn't seem to be any rhyme or reason, except *death*." Her words carried a thread of desperation, one he could understand.

Jonah appeared out of nowhere. "Because they don't understand the value of a life. Remember, we're fighting against those bred for war, who are lacking any form of empathy. To them it's simply a resource to be used. Now, are you both all right? I've got Dr. Aros standing by in case you need to talk to someone."

Franklin heard Senna's snort. "I'm fine, thanks. Franklin?"

"Good too," he answered even though he knew he'd see this in his dreams for the next little while. It wasn't something that happened in front of you without leaving some kind of scar.

"Report?"

"It was the last of the day's final batch," Senna replied. "He was clearly uncomfortable, and Franklin locked down the unit."

"The lockdown sequence was triggered. He knew we knew, and he started pulling at his clothes, tearing them. I saw the device and warned Senna. He tried to break out, then *poof*." Franklin wanted to forget the last bit, yet it was imprinted in his memory.

"Okay, we'll pull the vid feed. See if there were any further indications. Right now, downtime for both of you."

Jonah headed into the building, and Franklin pulled Senna to his side, locking her with his arm as she leaned into the support he offered.

"This isn't war, Franklin. It's carnage."

He couldn't help but agree.

*S*enna rifled through the files mounting up on the desk she'd taken to thinking of as her own. "There has to be some kind of connection." Since the man, Evan Illurida, had committed suicide in the scanning tube, she'd been trying to find a connection between him and what they knew of the children, those running the project, or even the money trail. Thus far, nothing came to light.

"He lists no family, was accepted as a colonist after his application, had no health issues listed. I don't get it, Franklin."

The man sitting opposite her was working on a remote pad, hunting through PolSearch—the crime search module used by the security services. "I don't have any hits either. He's not obviously connected to any of the other colonists and yet another dead end."

Not the first in their six-day search.

"When are Erin and David due back? She's better as this sort of thing." And the truth was she desperately needed someone with the abilities Erin had. Maylin was tied up with the other mission, Franklin was better at other aspects of the investigation, and she'd been trying to work through this wholly unfamiliar task.

"They were due back yesterday, but Jonah said they'd heard nothing in the last two days. He's getting frustrated and worried, Daniella is a cat on hot bricks, and Michael wants to go find him but is running the medical familiarization sessions with the Colonists."

She bit her lip. *Too many holes to plug with so few bodies.*

If only there were others to help take up the fight. "We're not much use to Jonah at the moment. What if we suggested we go look for David and Erin? They're supposed to be bringing in the reinforcements, and we need them now."

Franklin grunted. "Things are pretty quiet right now, so he might agree to that. Let's check when he pops in."

Senna looked down at the piles of paper. "I need a coffee," she declared and stood. It wasn't that she needed one, just something active to do. Waiting and flicking through sheaves of paper wasn't actively helping, and she needed to know she was making a difference.

Stalking from one end of the office space to the other, Senna lifted the carafe and refilled the coffee. It was hot and bitter. Pretty horrible actually, she thought, sipping the brew, but anything was better than sitting around.

Franklin stood and framed her shoulders with his hands. "It'll be okay."

Not helping.

"Look, I know you're frustrated and sick of sitting here." Franklin turned her in his embrace. "But you know we all have our roles. We do what we can, we help in our own way. Sometimes we're the ones waiting, and sometimes we're the ones doing."

"But it isn't enough, Franklin. I should be out hunting down the children, or investigating something."

Then Senna slumped into his arms. "I sound like a wimp. Hell, I feel stupid and useless right now. I've always been busy." Her fingers curled around the sleeves of his uniform, reinforcing the dissatisfaction she felt at her current inactivity.

The door slid open and Jonah walked in. "Did I come at an inopportune time?"

Senna slipped out of Franklin's grasp and immediately felt the loss of his support. "No, Jonah. But I need to be doing something. With David and Erin still not back—"

And here, the grave look on Jonah's face deepened, firm etches of lines on his face. "I actually planned to talk to you about that."

Jonah moved around the desk, settling in Senna's chair as if born to the position of command. "I expected them back the day before yesterday. There's been complete radio silence from them, which isn't totally unusual, however, given there've been no further incursions, I'm..." He dragged in an unsteady breath. "Well, I'm uncomfortable with this. I need you two to go out, under cover, and find them. Find out what's gone on, and if necessary, extract them. I can't spare anyone else to support you, so you'd be on your own."

The anxiety curling in her chest released, like a chain unwound on a wheel. But while she was ready and able, it wasn't just her. They were a team now, her and Franklin. "Franklin?"

"Yeah."

The single word sealed their agreement to the mission. "Where did they go, and how long do we have?"

Jonah gazed at her. "You're sure you want this?"

If there was a flutter of butterflies in her belly, she ignored it. "Yeah."

"We aren't exactly sure where they are. We know the general location of Homewoods, but not much else. Get them out, get me people, and do it quickly, because the calm isn't going to last."

Jonah rose, turned to Franklin. "Above all, don't take chances. The two of you are as valuable as the rest of my crew."

Senna blinked, unsure if the message was for both of them, but it felt like an order.

CHAPTER 13

Franklin hefted the box into the vehicle. It looked like an average ground car, sounded like an average ground car, but that's about where the average ended. Carefully built to resemble something that came off the showroom floor, it was reinforced, had tires that didn't burst, and a system for guidance and steering that was the love child of some stealth aircraft.

Senna shoved the sleeping sacks onto the back area, obscuring the ammunition rack which replaced the seat, they had folded up.They'd already fueled the anonymous looking car, all three long-range tanks topped up so they'd be able to get further. The additional armament increased the weight but not enough to hamper the fuel efficiency. They'd stashed money too, both agreeing that would be better than traceable card payments should they need to bribe civilians or purchase items.

Closing the hatch, Franklin peered over the top of the car. "Ready?"

Senna turned back to the building. "One more thing." She disappeared inside before returning with a hot bottle and a cooler bag. "Some traveling food."

He laughed at her triumphant look, then rounded the car to climb into it. They each latched their belts, and he depressed the ignition button and pulled away from the building. By their estimation, they had a three-day trip ahead of them, stopping only for the necessary breaks and taking turns to drive.

They drove to the wide, angular gates of the base. The first set opened wide and the car slid through. At the second set, tensions seeped. This was where they might find evidence of attempted entry. But the third gate, that opened to the wider and infinitely wilder world.

That no one waited outside was a blessing, but it also had Franklin worrying that someone might be watching. "What if there's a child watching?"

"They'd have to be quick to keep up with us, and once we accelerate—"

"We already know they've got adults to assist. What if there's one driving a vehicle?" he muttered.

"Just waiting around at this gate in case we decide to drive through on a secret mission?" She quirked her brow.

When Senna put it like that, his ruminations sounded ridiculous, except they didn't. "Yeah, you're right. But even though it sounds ridiculous, we have to be aware and cautious."

Senna nodded. "We do, true. But unless they've managed to place a tracker on the vehicle or someone tipped them off—and let's be honest, we've played safe not telling anyone except Michael, Jonah, and Daniella—who would know? Even Clarissa wasn't included in order to keep the information limited."

Sliding down into the seat, Senna nodded, sliding a pair of binocglasses on and scanning the surrounding areas.

"Anything?"

"Not a thing that I can see. The only thing that's obscuring my view is the rubble of the buildings razed in the early days. Nothing else. No movement and no warm life signs."

"Good." He punched the accelerator, welcoming the forces that pushed him back into the seat. "Once we're in the open countryside, get some shut-eye. I'd like to get a couple of hours under the belt before we change over."

"You know, I was checking the maps again, and I'm sure I can find a quicker route. When we looked at the roads, we kept to the main highways, but even though this is a pretty heavy machine, I think some of the backroads would let us cut maybe another twelve to fifteen hours."

He considered her words. "Tell me more."

"Well, at Caningham the highway forks, and if we turn to the left, we're on the old Cross-Country highway. We go north from there."

In his mind, he checked her calculations and impediments. "Towns?"

"There's a couple, so we can take breaks. They're small enough that any children will be noticeable, particularly of the warrior kind."

"You're pretty good at this strategy thing, aren't you, Senna?"

She colored at his words. "I like to plan. It's like a game or a puzzle. I've always been good at them."

"I would never have guessed."

She laughed, and it intrigued him.

"Where I grew up, I was looking for things to keep my mind active," she continued. "This was the answer as far as I was concerned, and I spent hours reading, doing puzzles, and drawing."

"Drawing?"

"Yeah. I guess that's what made me so good with picking off clues. You could say I've been training my whole life. But what about you? You're awesome with a rifle, and even though you tried to get yourself killed, which I might add gave me a heart attack, you've got mad fighting skills."

Now that did surprise him. "You were concerned?"

Her face took on the look of a deer being stalked. He almost laughed at the way her eyes widened, and her mouth opened, shut, then opened again. "I... Yes! I was. I mean you're a friend, or were, sort of."

"Sort of, huh?"

But the teasing died away as she swallowed hard. "I saw what you did, Franklin. That night of the attack? It was both brave and foolish."

Tears glistened on her lashes, and she blinked rapidly. "You, uh, didn't tell me about your skills though."

Staring at the road ahead, he inhaled. "There's not really much to it. At school I showed an aptitude. My coach picked me out, trained me. When I left and joined the corps, I was shunted into a specialist advanced frontal assault unit for a while. They trained us well, then I slid sideways into the guards. Told me the added benefit would assist my charge to remain safe. The usual stuff."

His gut churned. He wanted to tell her everything, but would she turn away once she knew the full extent of his background?

He cleared his throat and continued, because they couldn't have any kind of relationship without honesty. "When you grow up like I did..." He licked his lips. "My father, I told you about him? Well, I spent as much time away from home as I could after my mother died. Took every advantage I could scrape together. The coach saw a scrapper and honed me. Gave me the entry I needed to escape the old man."

Senna stared at him as her hand reached out and touched his. The small act warmed him.

"You made yourself the man you are, Franklin." In her eyes he read not the pity he'd always expected but triumph. "Never be ashamed of that. You've already achieved more."

Uncomfortable with the intimacy of the moment, he pushed his mind back to the conversation they had been having. "With the rifle, I've always been interested in devices like them." He stole a quick glance at her from the corner of his eyes, noting her tiny smile as if she understood what he was doing. "It's not like I'm some weapon nut though. I trained on as many as I could during my time in the assault crew, learned how they work. How to repair them, because that understanding makes you a better marksman. Built a couple of my own." His hand caressed the tiny pistol on his hip, his first and arguably the best one yet. "I'll show you later, if you'd like."

His glance this time found her staring, mouth wide open. "You built a gun?"

"A couple, but it's my little one that's still my fave. Fits my palm and built of plasti-carbon fiber. Holds only five bullets, but she's true, small, and even better, waterproof."

"And you still put yourself down," she murmured. "You're a wizard, Franklin. An absolute wizard."

⸙

Two days passed, and Senna ached. The car that had seemed quite comfortable at the beginning of their mission now resembled a war zone. They'd only stopped for the necessary ablution breaks and to change over drivers. Food was consumed on the road and the wrappings discarded into a container, but the blanket they'd draped over themselves while sleeping during the day tangled into the headpiece of the seat.

Drink containers filled the rear floor, mounded over their personal packs.

Senna stretched as much as possible. "We must be close." She yawned.

Franklin rubbed at his red eyes. "Yeah. I checked the map on my last break and calculated the distance. I'd reckon in the next hour or two we should start to see signs of habitation." He craned, looking between the trees, and Senna winced, jostled by the ruts in the dirt road. "I'm not surprised that some chose to come here though. It's..." He seemed to search for the right word. "...calming."

"I know. It's cool and dark, and I feel like I should be whispering. And that makes no sense, right?" She felt the smile stretching across her face. "I've not spent a lot of time out of the city except, you know, during the battle. This is totally different. Like being in another world."

"Yeah. I like it."

She couldn't contain her nod. "Me too."

Silence stretched as they made their way up the road until a rumble grew.

Senna leaned forward, peering. Itching settled between her

shoulder blades, and she reached out, her hand sliding over his wrist. "Franklin? I think we should stop. Get off the roadway."

He grunted but pulled the vehicle off to the left, arrowing it between the trees until he was sure they were obscured from the roadway.

"We need to clear the tire tracks," he whispered, and she nodded her agreement. "Stay here, and keep an eye out."

She watched as he picked up a spy-ear and slid it in, then slid one into her own ear, ensuring they'd have the ability to communicate no matter the circumstances.

Heart beating like a timpani, she waited, watching his movement, all the time aware he was keeping an eye up the road, as he rubbed at the tracks with a branch he'd snapped from a tree before retreating. It was just in time as a truck, loaded with warrior children, passed by, followed by a second and a third, but not before she spied David and Erin in the front of the second truck.

Finger to the depression point, she spoke quietly. "We have to get them out."

"We can't use the vehicle, they'll hear it and see it."

Senna scratched her head. "The jet packs. Are they limited or long-range battery units?"

His grin warmed her as he gazed through the window of the vehicle, opening it so she could step out. "Long-range." He popped the back of the vehicle, and they unpacked what they needed, including several pieces of armament and skinsuits capable of repelling munitions. Senna stashed some sleeping gas balls into her pocket.

"We'll have to be quick," she said, climbing into the skinsuit then sliding into the jetpack.

A solar charger went into Franklin's pocket, then assured they had everything they needed, they scurried to a clearing. Hands on the bars, they lifted off.

They sailed just above the treetops, hunting for the road, then keeping it in sight as they trailed the trucks.

The sun dipping below the horizon would assist in keeping their location from the view of any lookouts, but the trucks didn't go far, simply turning off some fifteen minutes later into an abandoned quarry.

Franklin and Senna set down about half a mile and moved in on foot, having discarded the jet packs. They noted the location though, unwilling to lose such valuable tools.

"Looks like they're setting up camp," she whispered as they crouched on the perimeter.

"Yeah, but where are David and Erin?" Two tents had been set up on the edge of the clearing as the children gathered around the fire.

"I'm not sure, but we need to go in and get them. It doesn't look like they've posted sentries. I'm quicker, and you're better with a rifle, so give me cover. I'm going to try the smaller tent first."

"Senna—" His gaze clouded.

She moved in, nearly whispering against his ear. "It makes sense, Franklin. They'll have them in a separate area, and I'll bet the big tent is the for the children. We've already seen they're adroit at certain kinds of strategy but lacking in others. I'm willing to bet this is one of those times, looking at the way they're sitting there."

Before he could say otherwise, she was off across the clearing. Senna kept her steps as light as she could, watching for rocks and stray sticks that might betray her if she stepped wrong, staying low, aware that every move made her more of a target.

Reaching the canvas structure, she took a moment to calm her breathing. Slowly, she moved so she was able to peer through the flaps.

With a trembling finger, Senna slid a flap to the side, widening the gap. David and Erin sat in the center of the tent and no one else appeared within.

She listened, scanning for the sound of footsteps, but there weren't any. Carefully, she rose, keeping an eye on the surroundings and moved within the tent.

David raised his head, mouth open. He was bruised, a trail of dark, dried blood from the corner of his lip to his chin. Erin didn't move.

Senna raised a finger to her lips, reminding him to stay quiet as she shuffled forward.

Reaching into her boot, she tugged out a knife and sliced through the knotted rope that tied him to the central pole before doing the same with Erin.

She moved close enough that her cheek touched David's. "Franklin is outside. We need to get out."

He nodded and scooped the unconscious Erin into his arms.

At the flap, Senna carefully peered, and sighting no one, she indicated he should move into the woods and held up three fingers.

One deep breath, then they dashed, silent and quick. "This way," she whispered and led David to where Franklin, waited.

"What happened?" Franklin demanded, and David grimaced.

Before anything more could be said, Senna poked Franklin in the side. "Later."

David repositioned Erin over his shoulder. They ran as fast and quietly as they could, everyone aware they needed to put as much distance as possible between them and the children.

Once they were back in the clearing where Franklin and Senna had stashed the jetpacks, Senna turned, and David lowered Erin to the ground. She checked the woman's injuries, satisfied they weren't, as far as she could tell, life-threatening.

There wasn't time for them to do more than catch a few minutes rest, and Senna demanded, "What the hell happened?"

"They were waiting for us. We'd almost got to Homewoods when they appeared. They must have worked out where we were going, because they had a roadblock set up. We never made it. I still don't know if Astrid and Jude are bringing reinforcements or found another way. But when they got us, they held us until they were joined by their illustrious leader. We're half-right though. Lilly is a main player, but the head is her mother."

Senna blinked at David's words. "I thought Senator Montaine's wife was dead."

David's laugh lacked any mirth. "She is and she isn't. I don't know when you saw us—"

"We were about an hour or two out of Homewoods when the convoy passed us by."

David stared at her. "What?"

"Three trucks. We followed you from not far out of Homewoods."

"We'd been on the road for several hours. So, they took us I thought toward their base south of here. Obviously not." He closed his eyes. "Erin wasn't caught straight away. She tried to get word to the reinforcements, but they caught her two days ago. They knew there were two of us, they'd been told we were together."

David ran an unsteady hand over his wife's face. "They beat her in front of me, and there wasn't any way I could help. They kept us in cells next to each other." His voice broke, and when he looked at Senna, her heart quivered.

"They'll pay, David. But first we have to get out of here. Before they track us down. But Montaine's wife. I need to know."

"The woman who is Montaine is a different body but the same person. They're perfecting the process of the brain transplants. Taking someone who's dying and transferring them into another body. Lilly spilled the truth when they were questioning me."

"God! We need to get back then. Tell Jonah and Daniella. What about the reinforcements? Are they still coming?"

David shrugged. "I don't know. We didn't get that far."

"No, of course not." She hesitated for a moment. "Is there another way back?"

David nodded.

"Good. We get to the vehicle and get out of here. We need to get back and see if Astrid and Jude's people got out too."

Franklin and Senna picked up the jet packs, hefted them so they wouldn't leave them behind, and David gathered up Erin again. "The vehicle is about a mile or so away. We need to move quick and stay away from the main road."

"We only crossed the road once, so if we head straight for it now, and wait for a break, we should be able to make our way through the forest. It'll cut off some time if we go direct."

Senna considered Franklin's words. Given David's condition and that he was carrying Erin they would be slower. "Franklin, take Erin."

"No. I'll take her," hissed David.

There wasn't time to argue, so with a look at Franklin, brows narrowed and a worried look on his face, they headed out.

Night fallen during the rescue and subsequent discussion of tactics. The dark was all encompassing, and they had to move much more slowly. Much as Senna wanted to rest, and knew David probably needed it, there wasn't time. They set a brutal pace, and once across the road, they continued in a straight line in almost silence. The only noise that betrayed them was the crunch of leaves and sticks underfoot.

Sometime later, David called a halt. "Water, do you have any?"

Franklin took Erin while Senna extended the small canteen she pulled from her hip. "Let us help you, David."

He drank, throat moving with each swallow. "No. My responsibility."

"But you're in no condition—" added Franklin.

"She's my *wife*." David wiped his brow. "Look, I can't explain it, but I carry her, okay?" The bravado melted away, and his voice quavered, "Senna, shouldn't she have come around by now?"

Senna had pondered that too. "The jostling won't be helping, but I'll take another look when we get to the vehicle. At this point we're out of options. It's probably something simple like a concussion." The only thing was, as David had pointed out, the longer she was out, the worse the condition could likely be, and concussion was never simple. They all knew that.

As David bent to pick his wife up again, Erin roused, "David? Where are we?" Erin's voice was groggy, but the concern that had written itself over David's face melted away.

David screwed his face, tears dribbling down his cheeks. "Oh baby, I was so worried about you."

"My head hurts. Lots. And where are we? Is that Franklin and Senna?" She tried to shove up, but Senna crouched down and stilled her.

"Let me take a quick look at you." In her makeshift pack, she had a small torch, and she pulled it out and shined it in the woman's eyes. Her pupils were dilated, but there was no sign of blood. "Stiffness, nausea?"

"My stomach is a little uncertain, but I don't remember much about how we got here."

Senna nodded. "Okay, David's going to carry you. We need to get to the vehicle—"

"But how did we get here in the middle of the forest? The last I remember is…"

David swooped in and kissed her, and Senna looked away, uncomfortable with the caress between the couple.

"We have to move, honey. I'll explain once we're safe."

The sound of movement had Senna's head snapping up. "We have to move. Now!"

It might be wildlife or the children. Whichever way, she didn't want to see it, especially since they had two injured with them, making them more of a target. Senna hurried them on, Franklin at the front while she cleared the rear.

Whatever the sound was, it didn't follow, and they reached the vehicle with no further problems, although they were all breathing heavily from exhaustion. Erin was the worst, and after another quick check over, Senna dosed her with a light painkiller and water, theorizing it was better to do something than nothing at all.

They rearranged the vehicle so Erin and David were in the back, the munitions in easy reach, and dumped the unimportant items into the forest. There wasn't room, and they could be replaced, unlike the couple in the back seat.

Franklin took up position as the driver while Senna and David worked out their route.

An old, rough logging road wound in the direction they needed to go, so they headed that way. It was the dead of the night, and no one shared the old road. Within an hour, they'd reached the other side. At the highway, Franklin stopped the vehicle. "If we go that way, we might run into the children."

It was a fear Senna shared.

"True, but it's our only other option. We know back the way you came leads us almost directly to their camp," David pointed out, and Senna's stomach curdled at that possibility.

"We don't have much of an option though, do we? I can't be caught again, Franklin. None of us can afford that. I vote we take the chance, get as far as we can. They won't be checking, they don't of an evening. It's as if they don't have the stamina or—"

Senna turned her head to Erin, aware of the importance of that statement, even if no one else was. "What? What do you mean by *they don't of an evening*?"

Erin twisted in the seat, releasing a hiss of obvious discomfort. "They almost shut down. The adults with them take over minimal control, but their job is mainly to drive and direct. None of them are military trained though, so..." She shrugged, and Senna closed her eyes, offering thanks for this tiny grain of information.

"Have we ever seen them active at night?" she wondered aloud.

Franklin simply frowned. "Not a lot. We had the massed attack on the base, but that's about it. I wonder if there are ranks of soldiers and ranks of others to do the more menial tasks. Some prepared for night maneuvers and others for day. That would make sense."

David gathered Erin closer at Franklin's words, at least until she yowled with pain.

Senna tossed the information about in her mind. *Some created to fight during the day but unable to be useful in the night, while others the opposite. Splitting resources. Perhaps that could be used to our benefit.* So long as the intel was sound, of course.

"We have to get back as quickly as we can and tell Jonah what we've learned," Senna said.

"I agree. So, highway?"

"Yeah. Let's get back to base as fast as we can."

CHAPTER 14

*T*he journey took two days, and Franklin knew Senna was concerned about Erin. She dispensed analgesics and fretted. They pushed the vehicle hard, but by the end of the second day the base was a beacon on the horizon.

"Thank heavens," he muttered, and Senna glanced at him. She didn't speak, but he could tell she agreed with his comment.

The vehicle ate up the road, a series of motley vehicles following the same path catching his attention.

"Stop!" called David, and Franklin looked around, stunned.

Nonetheless, he glided the vehicle to the side of the road and noted the collection followed suit. David and Erin were out of the car and hurried to the lead vehicle. He and Senna followed slowly.

David and Erin embraced a grizzled, older couple and introduced them as Astrid and Jude, and Franklin knew this was the crew coming to bolster the crews working night and day at the base.

"What the hell?" Astrid exclaimed after David had introduced her. The older woman's graying hair was scraped back in a messy topknot.

"We were jumped just outside the township. We haven't yet managed to get word to Cam," said David as he dragged his hand through his hair. "I'm not sure they'll go further but…" He shrugged as waves of frustration rolled off Jude.

"We've got ways to contact them. Let them know," Jude, a grizzled man of indeterminate age, rasped, then returned to his vehicle. It looked like a wreck, yet the purr of the engine belied its state.

"How?" demanded Franklin, but the woman—Astrid—simply winked.

As they neared the base, they slowed, scanning for signs of incoming warriors, Franklin's hackles rose.

"I wonder if they've got the cargo onboard yet?" Jonah queried of Senna.

"They were taking a day or so, since the process of getting the colonists into the stasis pods is slow. I think once they cleared the medical process there was talk that they would be placed in family groups, their personal items loaded into the allocated containers."

The cars came to a halt and Franklin and David climbed down to confer with Astrid and Jude and how the next short while may proceed.

Without much further chatter, they broke away and headed back to their vehicle, Erin remaining in the back seat and David sliding in beside her.

The vehicle purred as Franklin touched a finger to the ignition point and they glided back onto the road, all the while aware that ahead someone might be watching.

They approached a bridge, the small river below full, thanks to the seasonal northern rains. The vehicle clattered on, crossing the river, and once they'd cleared it, he saw them—a knot of children waiting in silence at the second bridge, their stances wide, like conditioned fighters. Sentinels refusing them passage.

"Shit!"

Senna reached for her pistol. "I can take them."

He grunted, seeing only three. Behind him came the rustle of movement, and he guessed David had also pulled out his pistol. "There's more than that," Franklin muttered, and he noted others climbing from below.

He stamped on the brake, indecision warring inside.

Reverse and retreat. Wait for reinforcements.

Push onward. Drive through the mass, and hope we can shake them off before we reached the gates.

"We should stop, Franklin. What if they have Mother of Satan?" Senna's words exploded in his mind.

He growled with fury, threw the gear stick into reverse, and the car whined as he floored it, retreating to the bridge and off the other side. "Senna, get in contact with Jonah. We need reinforcements."

The car spun, a wild fishtail movement that sent them flying against the seat. Erin cried out, and David cursed.

"There's two hours until sunset. They're probably the daytime contingent. If we hunker down, we can wait them out." Erin groaned from the rear seat.

He considered her words. "Perhaps, but they may have reinforcements on the way. We need to move."

He spied Astrid and Jude and all the others loaded on the truck, and pulled alongside it. "We need to back up. There's a roadblock of sorts ahead."

Astrid's eyes narrowed. "Roadblock? What kind of blockage?"

"Children," Franklin groused.

"Hmm. They've got bio-tech, right? I might have something that will assist."

Franklin watched as Astrid ducked down then reappeared with an overlarge knapsack in hand, and they waited for her to dig in the bag and pull out a box. David had explained that she'd previously worked for Max-Corp, a communications and electronics company, and insisted she'd be as good as her word.

She fiddled with knobs, pressed buttons, then lifted the flap to show more buttons. It only took her a few minutes while they anxiously watched the children advance.

Franklin kept a close eye on their movements, preparing mentally for the attack to come. They stilled, faces frozen in surprise.

"That will give us a couple of minutes. We should get moving though," Astrid called.

Franklin couldn't explain how he felt, but nonetheless, he followed her instruction, and they moved the vehicles like a snake through the statue-like children. With everyone they passed, he stared. In their gazes he read hatred and fury, but they were as if frozen.

"How the hell did she do that?"

"I don't have a clue, but I'm sure glad she's on our side," breathed Senna.

"She's a wonder, isn't she? Saved our asses back with the copter," David offered from the back, reinforcing Franklin's own thoughts.

The last car cleared the second bridge as the children broke free of whatever had stopped them. Their movements were jerky, and Franklin pushed the vehicle faster, not intending to hang around long enough for them to regain their full capacity. He'd already seen what they were capable of.

They whizzed along, spearing toward the gates, but before they could make it, he glanced in the mirror to see the children were now running.

He pressed the accelerator all the way to the floor, opened the channel to the base. "Open the gates. We've got vehicles entering and we're under threat."

It was the best he could do, but the gates swung up, only about halfway, but enough for the vehicle and the truck to slide in before the gates clanged shut.

Gaining the second gate, he chanced another look in the rearview mirror and noted the children had stopped, fingers curling into the wire as their faces pushed against the mesh.

The frantic thud of his heart slowed, and he released the oxygen he'd sucked into his lungs, the exhalation deep.

"We made it," murmured Erin, and he grunted.

Thanks to Astrid and her magic box. He'd be sure to mention that to Jonah, and maybe he'd ask her to build one for him.

Senna sat on the steps in the gathering gloom. Having sent a message to Franklin, she hoped he'd join her.

The sound of footsteps had her scanning the horizon. Franklin made his way in her direction, his outline strong and sturdy. "Franklin."

He stepped up as Senna stood. "Hi."

Shyness overtook her, and she dipped her gaze to the floor. "I'm, uh... I'm glad you could come."

"There isn't anywhere else I'd rather be." The timbre of his voice rippled through her.

On the steps behind her was a bag of meals, prepared by herself from the mess and the MRE's she'd stashed for their mission. "Would you join me?"

His nod warmed the cold knot in her belly, and he took her arm once she'd scooped up the bag. The glasses and bottle clanked and he turned. "What's that?"

"I organized some dinner for us."

He didn't speak, but neither did he pull away. Senna wasn't sure if that was good or bad, but she was also aware he was probably feeling at sea.

"I thought we could go sit in the courtyard. I saw there were some seats there, and I hoped...that is, it would be nice to have dinner alone. Just the two of us."

Being the instigator wasn't something she'd ever done before, but with Franklin she was willing to take the chance.

"That sounds great," he said, and they walked slowly in the direction of the tables and chairs.

"Did you know, in ancient times courting couples would walk arm in arm in the twilight? I never really got that before."

"Is that what we're doing, Senna?" He stilled and she stopped.

I've said too much. "I... Uh, not necessarily. I was just making conversation."

He reached up, framed her face with one meaty hand. "Really?" There was an undefinable quality to his voice, like a siren's call.

The touch of his hand, featherlight on her skin, drugged her.

"Senna? What are we doing?" Franklin's voice whispered over her senses, pulling her in.

"I... I don't know."

"I want you, Senna."

Her heart lurched. *Want.* She knew that emotion well. "I want you too."

He closed the distance between them, the kiss so light it nearly didn't happen, but the intimacy of it was obvious.

The kiss ended quickly, a touch and a promise. "Let's go eat then."

Franklin curled his arm around her waist, locking her in step with him. He didn't restrict or demand, simply was there beside her.

He stopped at the first table. "This one?"

"Yeah."

The settled onto the seats, and she pulled out the glasses and bottle of wine she'd arranged from the Officer's Club. "Michael got this for us. I thought it might, you know, be nice."

Feeling like a fool, she reached in and tugged out the two beef stew meals. "I don't have the facilities to cook, so..." She shrugged but he smiled.

"My favorite."

Senna laughed. "I'm feeling foolish."

"Why?"

"Because I should be cooking you a meal, and setting an elegant table with a snowy white cloth. Instead, here we are with MRE's and a bottle of wine I organized someone else to get." Exasperation colored her words, but he laughed.

"Senna, we're on a base, with possible incoming at any time. You took the initiative, came up with the goods. Don't beat yourself up. You did good!"

He sounded so sincere that tears pricked. "I just wanted to do something special. To let you know I think you're special."

He leaned in, so his lips were mere millimeters away from hers, and his warm breath caressed her flesh. "You have. Thank you."

Sure he would kiss her, shock and a sense of loss assailed when he moved away. She might have mewled, and he smiled. "Soon."

She stared, aware her mouth was open. "Why?"

"Absence and all that. Let's be patient. Let this feeling grow, because anticipation is sweeter."

Argh! Her mind reeled, and she thought of a million retorts, but they were too late and beneath her.

Instead, Senna set about setting out the meal. Some cheeses Clarissa had sent to go with the wine and fruit. Delicious and succulent pears.

He popped the top on the stew and smiled. "How do we heat this?"

In the bottom of the bag was a small box, which she pulled out. It unfurled to reveal a small heater, and one by one she heated the stew and spooned it into bowls.

"I used to like stew, but it's getting a little old now."

He nodded. "I know. I mean, Clarissa makes a mean one, but I wish there was something edible in the mess hall, then there'd be an alternative."

"I guess we should be thankful we have an alternative. Those who've only got the mess..." Senna shuddered, and he laughed.

They finished the meal, washed it down with a glass of wine, and enjoyed each other's company for the next little while, but as the night wore on, the awareness between them grew.

Once they'd finished, he cleared his throat, and Senna couldn't contain the smile.

"Help me carry this back, Franklin?"

She dropped their items into a basket, and he hefted it easily. When Franklin held out his hand there was no other option but to accept it. Anything else would bely the question that had been asked.

At her building, he paused. "Are you sure?"

Senna reached for the basket as he frowned, then she laid it on the steps. "I was ready before you, Franklin. Don't make me wait longer."

The desire that had pooled spread, like a wave of delicious

hunger, so that every synapse yearned as they kissed. It was soft and drugging, but as they pulled away, the hint of fire remained.

Without another word, he lifted the basket and followed her up the steps to her floor. They moved along the concrete, feet tapping in unison, and as she reached for her door, the hunger roared. Senna's fingers shook as she swiped the card, fumbled, and it fell. She swore loud enough to make him snort as she fished around.

Card once more in hand, she concentrated, and the door opened. He pushed her in then followed. The basket fell with a thud to the floor as they reached for each other.

"Clothes…" she whispered as they came together, his mouth roaming over hers, seeking access to her mouth, and she opened for him.

He groaned and tugged at her shirt; restless, wordless demands for them to be naked. Her eyes fluttered shut as the carnality tore at her senses. Overload breached as the taste of him, heady and all male, surrounded her.

The rasp of his facial hair scored the flesh of her cheeks, and she didn't care. All she needed now was him, the slide of his skin against hers as he filled her.

"More," she demanded, tugging away, eyes opening as she reached for his uniform shirt. Buttons popped as she yanked, and his fingers burrowed beneath her t-shirt. He grasped the band of the material and pulled, causing Senna to raise her arms on a curse as she spied the miles of flesh. The material slid over her face and fell to the floor.

Senna put both hands on the shoulders of his shirt and pulled, watching with fascination as it slid, before the material caught on his wrists.

He laughed and the ripple of muscles dried her mouth. "Undo them," she rasped, reaching behind to pop her bra. It sagged and she pulled the cloth away, watching the dilation of his eyes as he fumbled with the hidden sleeve buttons.

"Like what you see?" she asked.

"Oh yeah, but if we keep up this speed, we're going to be over before we start."

She laughed, and once he'd finally divested himself of the shirt, she plastered herself against his chest, welcoming the heat and scent of him. "If this time is fast, then you'll have to promise me slow for next time, tiger," she whispered, laying her lips against his.

Her fingers caught his belt, unfastened it, and she worked at the button and snap of his pants. Franklin responded in kind so that soon the only layer of fabric between them was his underwear and the legs of their pants, held in place by boots. Senna toed hers off and watched as he bent, unfastened the long strings, then shucked them.

Arms entwined, they danced their way to the bedroom and fell onto the bed, hands grasping and sliding, their lips locked, and her senses wildly overexerted. Her nipples grazed the hard flesh of his pecs and she moaned.

He chuckled and rubbed against her.

She squeezed her eyes shut. "More, Franklin. Touch me."

Franklin muttered something and slid his hand beneath the band of her underwear, sliding them down until he covered her mound. His hand burning her, Senna couldn't hold back the buck or the moan that erupted from her throat.

His mouth, the wet suction of it on her breast, spiked her blood pressure. "More!"

One finger threaded its way between her legs, finding the moisture and sliding within, and she moved, giving him full and unfettered access to her core.

Franklin lifted away. "I want to be inside you, Senna. This is your last chance to tell me to stop." The rasping words betrayed his hunger, as did the graven features.

"I don't want you to," she whispered.

"Senna?" He slipped away, giving her a moment to regain her senses. She replied by shucking her panties and tossing them. "Come here."

He followed suit and climbed up her body. "You're already hot, and to be honest, I'm not sure I can last, Senna."

She hooked one arm over his shoulder. "Then don't."

"Wait. Protection?"

Senna laughed against his mouth. "No problems. We're safe."

This time their mouths clung as they came together. Franklin moved, positioning his cock against her. She wound her legs around his waist as he slid home, filling her, and the sensations came close to exploding her mind.

The movements turned frantic as the coil deep inside her belly demanded fulfillment. Her fingers found the wiry tendons of his shoulders, dug deep and clung. "Oh God," she cried, throwing back her head. A kaleidoscope of color burst behind her closed lids as she demanded more.

The quicker they moved against each other, every slide and grope fed the urgency. Senna panted as his lips slid down her throat. She arched, body reacting instinctively as the sudden deluge of orgasm ripped through her system.

She clung tight, holding him close as the start of his jetting began. He grunted, his fingers speared into her flesh to hold her close, and the scent of their passion wreathed them. Their bodies were slick from exertion as they released their frantic holds.

"I... Senna, I've never..."

His voice quavered, and she heard the surprise in his tone.

"Me either." That was something she'd need to investigate. Later, she promised herself, nestling into his embrace. After she'd had time to rest and recover.

Franklin lay there, gazing at the ceiling, amazed, if not a little shell-shocked, at the emotions that ran like a deep river through him. Senna snuffled in her sleep, curled around him as if he were some kind of security blanket.

The passion that had exploded between them had been overwhelming. Almost too much to cope with, and his first instinct was to rise and head to his own room.

"No," he told himself. He wasn't a quitter, and that smacked of cowardice.

Instead, he wondered about the next step. What would it take to form a lasting connection with this woman? She didn't appear to the be flowers and candy kind of woman—and he was thankful for that—but what to do next?

Would she demand some kind of relationship? Was he reading too much into it?

The restless emotions exhausted him until he too dropped off to sleep holding her close.

CHAPTER 15

"The colony ship is now loaded," Jonah stated. "The colonist's pods are secured into position, as is the cargo. Meteorology indicate that the launch window is clear and optimal, and the security is tighter than ever around the perimeter. We'll scramble the jets in prep, and they'll circle the ship in a concentric pattern, looking for any incursions."

Senna made notes in her pad, highly aware of Franklin sitting beside her, their knees brushing against each other. Every pass heightened her awareness, and it took a great deal of willpower to concentrate as much as her splintered mind was capable on the briefing.

"Senna and her team have carried out the final inspection of the cargo, and our reinforcements are looking for anything that would give us an indication of an imminent attack."

Jonah stepped back, and Daniella took the podium. "Well done, everyone. So far, we've managed to control information to only what had to be released. My team has been working hard, and beginning today, will release incorrect information widely as part of a concerted effort to protect the lift-off. The people are demanding information, and after the fact, we will release more, but as of now, we're announcing that primary launch date is one week from today."

Some in the room rose in their seats, the hubbub rising to levels unusual in such a briefing, as they shared their discomfort with the subterfuge.

Daniella held up her hand. "Just a moment, please. Consider why we're doing this. That ship is loaded with hundreds of colonists. Their safety is of primary concern. Should the children know that we plan to launch today, I believe—and so does the commander—that the base would be overrun." Her face was hard as she slammed them with the undeniable facts. "We cannot allow that, hence our choice to distribute misinformation. We are not allowing media in for the shuttle launch, instead focusing on creating a media program that will help us calm the populace and increase their support of the government in the first instance. We also believe that once the launch takes place, safely, that we will be able to broadcast our reasons and the majority of the populace will understand. Our first scheduled broadcast goes live in half an hour."

Without taking any questions, Daniella walked away from the podium and out the door.

"I don't know about the misinformation. I mean, people will question everything they say after they know the truth," the woman on Senna's left murmured.

Another commented, "Propaganda has been part of the battle environment for centuries. People will forgive, just like they always do. It just takes time."

Senna kept her own counsel, preferring to focus on Jonah standing up and taking control, both hands in the air to calm the chatter.

"I know some of you question the efficacy of our decisions. Hell, it's not been easy, but it's necessary." He pounded the desk, and Senna was intrigued by the changes that had been wrought in Jonah. Previously, he'd been happy to take orders, but now he washe'd become a polished and confident as a leader. "With the reinforcements we've secured over the last week or so, the level of base security has risen and we're once again in a position to go on the attack. And attack we will. I've drawn up plans for a multi-pronged mission which will be circulated later today. You're my best, the leaders of teams and men. In difficult circumstances, you've held the line, ensured the safety of the base, but now we have to ask more. More of you and your people, but we believe in you. Know that you are equal to the task that lies ahead. We have faith in you. Good luck and good hunting."

Now the room rose, buoyed up. There was no time for questions as Jonah left, but the mood had risen.

Senna stood and waited as Franklin did the same. As they moved toward the door, they were beckoned over by Jonah. "I need to talk to both of you."

Something in the pit of her stomach yawed. What could possibly be wrong now?

They trailed him into a small room, and he shut the door. "The security briefing raised a problem, and I need both of you to take control of the situation."

Senna waited, wondering what more things could arise.

"We think we've located a device, possibly a missile. I need people I can trust on the ground. Senna, I wouldn't be surprised if they haven't booby-trapped it, so you're my go-to."

She raised her hands to argue, but he stilled her with a firm shake of his head.

"Look, I'm not expecting you to disarm anything, but you and your team are the only ones trained with the scanners. I need you there when the demolition team arrives."

A weird kind of buzzing took up wing in her head. The responsibility he was laying at her feet was massive.

Jonah turned to Franklin, and dread pooled in her belly, seeing the sudden slump of Jonah's shoulders. "I need Franklin there with his particular skill set too. We're going to need snipers to cover the team, and Franklin, you're the best I know. I'm sending you both in with a handpicked team. We need to neutralize the threat, because they've already got their device in place, and while we'll have birds in the air, there's too much at stake. Senna, you and Franklin together are a force to be reckoned with."

Franklin straightened. "All right then. Details?"

"You leave as soon as your team is assembled. They're the best, guys. Just like you." Jonah shoved a document wallet into Franklin's hands. "Just be safe, okay?"

Jonah nodded, then he pushed the door open and they stepped outside.

CHAPTER 16

They hunkered down, and Franklin kept his fingers on his lips, indicating the need for silence as he watched the movement ahead. Three children—though more accurately, they looked like teens—hovered by the unit.

They seemed to be waiting, whether for an older person or some indicator, he couldn't say. Just that they were there and appeared uncomfortable.

He shuffled back, drew level with Senna. "There's three there, but I don't think they're the ones in charge," he whispered. Franklin could still peer around the block they sheltered behind. It was imperative that he kept them and the projection unit in sight.

"Why?"

"Because of their movements. See how they barely move near it? I'd be willing to bet their sole job is to keep an eye out, and they've been told to stay away. The one in charge is likely nearby, so we're going to have to be careful."

Franklin motioned to the others, his eyes scanning the whole time, looking for threats. He moved them back, around the corner, and posted a watch.

"We're in the right location. The intel was on the money, but we've got at least three guarding it. I'm thinking the one who is trained to fire is nearby. You wouldn't place something like this without them being ready. Gunther and Ian, find a position somewhere with views. I'm on the roof and so is Irbam. Senna, your job on my cue is to scan for anything that might cause us a problem. Fawcett, Carrington, and Ellesdarm, eyes open. Any hostiles, you know the drill." He'd worked with them before and knew they'd protect Senna. That just left the two in charge of disarming any threats, including the launcher. Hopefully, it was that simple.

They passed around the canteen of water and drank deeply as they centered themselves. His team was the best. They all knew how to achieve their aims. All they needed now was luck and good timing.

Ellesdarm, on the watch, hissed. They rose, melting into the shadows of the building as the three were replaced by three more.

Franklin slid to the corner, watching the movements. With barely a word, the children who'd been watching handed over the guardianship, and Franklin cursed their timing. The sun was still high in the sky, and who knew how long these children would be on watch?

Senna touched his hand, and for a moment, he blinked, aware she'd snuck up on him. "What do we do?" she asked.

He glanced over his shoulder at her. "Wait."

They settled in, finding a grated sewer that allowed them to hear and see without being spied. One hour passed, then another. The team waited patiently, aware that acting in haste could be life-threatening.

As the sun finally slid below the horizon, he pushed the grate aside. and one by one, they slid from the depths. He waved two fingers to the west, and the men he'd chosen to survey the field bled into the night.

Irbam gave a single nod, then, on silent feet, he headed off to find a position on a rooftop.

One last look over his shoulder, then Franklin moved away, knowing Senna would be careful. Responsible. Anything else didn't bear consideration.

The inner-city region where they'd been called to find the missile was quiet. Rubble—left over from one of the children's attacks most likely—littered the ground, and he sought a building with an external ladder. Found one and pulled on the metal. It clattered, setting his teeth on edge. He risked a look, and the palpitations of his heart settled when no one came to see what caused the noise.

A buzz in his headset told him the team was coming online. *Good, I can keep track of the mission.*

Three floors were nothing, his heartrate barely impacted by the climb, and he wrestled himself over the edge of the building. He tugged the ladder into the retract position and waited. Every second of the wait an eternity. Finally assured nothing would get up there after him, he moved to the edge nearest the missile with stealthy moves.

Tugging the rifle off his shoulder, he changed his sight filter so it didn't reflect any light but read heat signatures of those waiting by the device. He would monitor his people. He knew that right now they'd be donning their munitions-proof vests.

"Move into position," he murmured into the spy-ear.

He watched Senna, with slow but purposeful movements, maneuver into the agreed location, just out of view of the children. They'd need a minute or two, to assure themselves that they'd eluded detection, and to reposition now that he was in a better position, before making the call for her to proceed.

The others followed suit, sliding in behind her.

Time ticked by. One minute. Another. He barely breathed, hoping for the best but expecting the worst, just as he'd been trained.

Senna's comm clicked. "I'm not close enough, Franklin. Another couple of meters and—"

"Not yet. We don't want to spook them." His fingers curled around the trigger, breathing shallowly in case he needed to fire.

From the corner of his eye, he discerned heat signatures. Ones he didn't know. *Shit!*

"Don't move, Senna. We've got incoming."

"*What?*"

"Get down. Hunker down as low as you can." Now he sighted

them. Five moved, and he wanted to scream. Instead, he tagged the others. "Movement. I've got the front."

"Next," muttered Irbam, and he knew there'd be no miss. Irbam was nicknamed *Irbam the Deadly* because his marksmanship was exceptional. The others would take their chances on who they'd pick off.

"On my mark," he muttered.

In his mind, he counted. *One. Two. Mark.*

A *ping* echoed and the first went down. Two others swiftly before he checked on Senna again, horrified to note she'd moved into the open, pistol in hand.

"Senna! Get down!" He stood up, ready to run to the edge and stop her.

Too late!

"*Franklin, help m—*" The words cut off. All that remained was the *oof* as she was propelled to the ground.

Her red heat signature exploded in his viewfinder, and he knew what he saw was the echo of blood. "Senna!" he bellowed. The firing from the others seemed to go on forever, every twang an insult to his excoriated mind.

Instinct warred. *Get down there and save her!* His mind countered with *save them all.* Training won as he glanced in the viewfinder.

A phalanx of children approached. At least twenty, he thought, but that would be a wild guess. *We've been set up.*

Eyes stinging, Franklin lined up the missile, aware he had at most moments to ensure it wouldn't destroy the ship.

He heard the cries of the men on the ground calling out to him. "They're taking the others. Including Senna," Irbam called.

I have to block it out. Use my training. Senna or the ship. He knew his job and would do it. But the cost would surely destroy what remained of his soul.

Dropping the eyepiece and searching hastily, Franklin lined up the launcher, seeking the trigger. One place on the base that he knew was sure to destroy it.

His finger squeezed just a little as he exhaled, then completed the task.

The ground shuddered, dropping him to the floor as a hand wound around his shoulder, spinning him.

Franklin came up, throwing the rifle to the side with a snarl of fury.

Hands flew in rapid succession as he fought. Hatred and rage searing every part of his being. "I'll kill you for this," he snarled, planting his fist. It connected, the crunch of bone marrying with the sweet spurt of blood. "You'll pay for what you've done!" The howl erupting from his soul.

He plowed his fist again as his opponent fell to the floor. The haze of red obscuring his vision melted away, and he dropped to the floor, his hand sliding over his face as loss and horror enveloped him. Tears burned as his chest heaved. *Senna.* His beautiful Senna. Shot. Hurt or dead, he didn't know, but the pain surrounded him.

After a short while, Franklin rose, wiping mucus and blood from his face as much as the tears. "Senna?"

"Unknown. But they took her and the explosives guys. We were sold out, Franklin. Some bastard passed us bad intel."

He knew that now. But by God they'd better watch out, because his fury knew no bounds.

*C*oming to was a bitch. Senna more than ached, her side radiating pain and heat. She reached for the injury, hissing as her hand slid down to discover the wetness. investigating the wound site in the dark. Clearly whatever hit her hadn't stayed, catching her side on the fleshy area of her hip.

Cautious movements ended in more pain, but at least she could move and the wound site didn't pulse blood, though it seeped more than she'd like.

"Senna?"

"Yeah," she said, but nausea threatened to overcome her. The bile in her throat hot and sour. "I've been shot."

"We know. After they shot you, Franklin and his men took out most of them when the missile exploded. At least, I think that was Franklin's work. They'd grabbed you, probably to take you prisoner, and we managed to pull you out of the pile of bodies—"

"Wha—"

He stopped her abruptly, sliding a hand over her mouth.

Footsteps, loud and frantic, rushed past. In the darkness all she could make out was the shine of the man's eyes.

Light footsteps. Children.

Time passed and someone in the place they hid shifted, the movement slow and almost soundless. "Where are we? Who else is here?"

"In a sewer. I'm Fawcett. Carrington didn't make it. Ellesdarm is further up the pipe. He's the one that saved us. We climbed into the first sewer we could find with loose screws. They didn't see us in the panic after the missile went bang, so we grabbed you and moved. It's not safe really, but we needed time for you to regain consciousness. Now I need to check your wound. See how bad it is."

"Bad enough, but survivable at the moment."

Senna guessed the use of a light at this point wouldn't be useful, and though she was aware that she'd sustained enough physical damage to be a long-term threat to her health, it would be nothing to what the warrior children would do to them if they were found. She shifted with a hiss toward the grating, stopping only when the stamp of many feet echoed a little too closely for comfort.

We have to get out of here. If only Ellesdarm could read minds. With a sigh, she let go of consciousness.

She dozed, waiting for time to pass, and the dim rays of sunlight woke her. The ache radiated, and her body warmed as the first tendrils of infection flared.

"We need water, food, and I think there's an infection setting in," she said, and caught sight of Fawcett, his face bloodied and bruised, one eye a puffy mass. His arm hung uselessly.

"We're stuck here until the day passes," Ellesdarm murmured.

The urgent need to empty her bladder warred with the pain and fuzziness invading her mind. "What's down that way? Is there any way out?" She pointed to the rear of the cave.

"We didn't really look that far. It's a sewer, and we don't know the layout."

She reached for her bag and sighed when she discovered it missing. "My bag?"

"Didn't see it," whispered Fawcett, and she watched as he moved restlessly on the ground.

"How bad are your injuries, Fawcett?"

"Dislocated shoulder, maybe a broken leg too. Bruising and so on. I'll live."

She squeezed her eyes shut, willing her mind to whir to life. Two with reasonably significant injuries. One who appeared unharmed. What was the best option?

"Ellesdarm, are they running regular patrols past here or just when the opportunity comes?" He'd been awake for some time and would have a better idea, she theorized.

"Irregular. Sometimes it's a single individual, then at others..." Ellesdarm shrugged. "Why?"

"Neither of us is going to be able to set any records. Fawcett's got a suspected broken leg and me... Look, we need to get word to the base that we're still alive. Everyone will be focused on the launch later—"

"It took place last night."

"Wha..." Reality impinged. Of course they'd launched. Jonah had indicated hours when they'd left the base, and that time had come and gone. Senna just hoped it had gone smoothly.

"Okay, even so, they'll be busy re-grouping. We need assistance out of here, but if they can use the sewer system, we can do that covertly. You need to get back, report, and get us help. We'll stay here. Wait for assistance."

She read the shock on his face.

"You're our only hope. One person uninjured has more than a chance, and we can't leave Fawcett here alone."

"But how…"

"We wait until their patrol is complete. Check to make sure the way is clear, then you run until you can blend. There's a safe house on Vernal. The old bakery. Get there and they'll assist you. You just have to be careful. Don't get caught or we're all in trouble."

He nodded.

"Strip off your uniform shirt and we'll wipe it in the muck. Get some on your face too." The heat of the day intensified, and perspiration dripped down her back as she gave directions to him. "Leave the canteen and your munitions pack here," Senna added.

Ellesdarm shuffled and divested under her instruction as a thought occurred to her.

"Do you have a first aiders kit?" she asked.

He shook his head, and the sudden burst of hope plummeted.

The stamp of feet nearby shut them all up, and she waited, waited, and waited some more. Urgency growing inside her chest, she needed to know what was happening but couldn't take the chance that movements would betray them, so she waited.

The minutes ticked by slowly until she heard the sound of those beyond moving off. "Check, and if it's clear, go. Don't look back, Ellesdarm."

He shuffled closer to the grate, peered out, then turned. "I'll send help." Ellesdarm shoved at the grate, which opened with a grinding whine, shoved it back into place, then with a last harried glance, he set off.

"Think we have a chance?" Fawcett asked.

"He's our only one," she replied as she turned her attention to Fawcett. "Let's hope he's up to the task."

The only thing she knew for sure was Franklin knew these guys and vouched for them. It had to be enough, because the weight of their survival lay on it.

"Let's hope he can save us," Senna said with a grimace.

ranklin fumed and fretted. He'd seen them grab Senna, and he was sure her life was in danger. The only thing was, they'd found the remains of Carrington but there'd been no sign of Ellesdarm, Fawcett, or Senna.

The youngster who'd attacked him was still out cold when the blast and lighting show of the launch occurred.

He'd glanced up then swore.

With care, he'd strung the youngster over his back and abseiled down the ladder to the ground, Irbam meeting him below. "What a fuck up!"

Franklin snarled in response, "They've got Senna, and the others."

"Carrington was left behind, poor buggar. He got caught in the blow after you destroyed the missile. He's not going to be easily recoverable."

Franklin ran an unsteady hand through his hair. "We have to find the others."

Irbam shook his head. "We have to get back and report. We did what we came to do, the shuttle went off, and given there were no secondary explosions, I'm taking it the launch was successful."

"I'm not leaving Senna—"

"We have to get back to base, Franklin. According to Jonah, she's a professional. Knows the ropes. And Jonah will—"

"She's the woman I love, Irbam." The words tumbled out, and he privately acknowledged they were the truth. He'd just never told her, always sure somehow there would be time. Now it had come and gone, and his fear of commitment had stolen that chance away.

"Ah, damn!" muttered Irbam, shaking his head. "Look, I understand, but you have to return to base now. We don't know where they took her, or even if she's not buried under that rubble somewhere, and all our work and loss won't fix things if you get caught."

Franklin cast his glance over the remains of buildings, the one he'd been on at the time of the explosion, wavering uncertainly, windows smashed, and all around there were smoking ruins.

If she were there... Franklin shuddered.

Irbam was right, yet Franklin felt nauseated at the thought of leaving, just in case she was still here somehow. *And you know that's extremely unlikely. You saw them shoot her, then grab her.* His mind almost splintered with both those memories.

Franklin rearranged his load, and Irbam pointed at the youth on his back. "What are you planning to do with him?"

"He's a present for Jonah," snarled Franklin as he started moving away, although inside him, the tearing sensation of loss stole away everything except raw determination.

CHAPTER 17

*D*elirium set in. Noises and sounds. Senna swore she heard Franklin's voice, but the thud of her head and the roiling of her belly beat her into submission. Once again she plunged into the dark, where surely she was roasted over a hot fire.

Movement and sounds again, and she rose up through the layers, hearing the beep of a machine and feeling soft hands on her body. The weight of her eyes refused to allow Senna to open them, and the sudden, gasping sensation of breathlessness had her clawing at her throat, her heart thudding wildly then not at all, a whine from a machine filling her senses. Voices yelled, and pain radiated inside her head and chest as something forced itself in. She coughed, and her body arched up, acting on its own.

"We've got her back." Someone draped a mask over her face.

Senna's fingers clenched for the vile-smelling item, trying to grab it away, then she dropped like a stone, back into the dark.

*S*enna opened her eyes, mouth dry and swollen, her entire body aching yet weak. "Where am I?"

An unsteady hand touched the side of her face. The scent and shape she knew. "You scared me, Senna. We found you after Elles-darm raised the alarm. You and Fawcett were in a pretty bad way when we found you two days after the launch. The fever..."

With determination, she crept her hand to Franklin's, her side screaming with the effort, and she panted before letting go. "What happened to me?"

"Your heart nearly gave out as they were prepping you for surgery. They hit you with a massive dose of adrenaline to restart it. Then they wheeled you into surgery. The infection was deep, Senna."

"But I'm here." She licked her dry lips. "Can I have something to drink?"

Franklin turned away and returned with a cup. "Drink slowly."

Only able to manage a few swallows, Senna held the moisture in her mouth and let it refresh the dry tissues before swallowing.

"The colony ship?"

He snorted. "Yeah, we got it off safe and sound. The media circus is doing its thing, and the people have forgiven our carefully constructed stories."

"That's good." Now exhausted, she lay back, closing her eyes until his hand gripped hers tightly.

"Senna?"

Eyes growing heavy, it was all she could do to remain awake and answer. "Hmm?"

"Don't go to sleep yet. I want to tell you something."

But she was already dozing and let go of awareness.

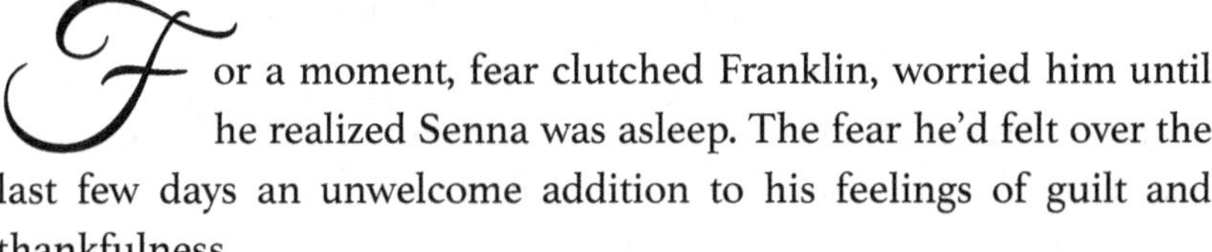

For a moment, fear clutched Franklin, worried him until he realized Senna was asleep. The fear he'd felt over the last few days an unwelcome addition to his feelings of guilt and thankfulness.

"Dammit," he muttered as the door opened to admit Clarissa.

"She woke?"

He glanced at the woman standing in the doorway. "Yeah. For a couple of moments." He moved, uncomfortably aware of the woman's focus on him.

"But not long enough?" She advanced and touched a soft hand to his shoulder. Under normal circumstances Franklin would have toughed it out. But today wasn't normal and he'd almost lost her. *Twice.*

"No. I was too slow." He shoved his hands deep into his pockets.

"She'll make a full recovery now, Franklin. Another opportunity will come up. Michael said she was pretty sick, but he got most of the infected tissue cleaned up and the antibiotics will do the rest. He does want to drain the wound itself until he's sure they got everything, then they'll tidy it up."

Franklin pulled his hands out of his pockets, clasped them on his knees, and looked at Senna, imploring her to wake again. "I'm lost, Clarissa. I want to tell her how I feel, but I don't know how." Emotions he couldn't contain welled.

Clarissa rubbed his shoulder. "All you have to do is say the words, Franklin."

If only it were that simple and I was brave enough.

A sound at the door had him turning. Jonah stepped inside, and the room now felt crowded. "How is she?"

"Michael says she'll recover," Franklin answered, lips stiff and his emotions a ball of complication.

"Look, I know these last few days have been hard." Jonah squatted down beside Franklin as Clarissa left them alone.

"She nearly died, Jonah. The woman I love." He hated that he wasn't in control of his emotions, the fury that coursed dashed down by the terror he'd experienced when he'd found her limp body, burning to the touch. "I should have known!"

Jonah sighed, a long, drawn-out exhalation which betrayed his frustration. "We all know the risks, Franklin."

"*I don't care!*" His bellow had his long-time friend rearing back in surprise. "I..." Franklin shook his head, trying to clear the fog which filled him.

"You need time, but I can't give it to you, not right now. We need you. You've got to pull yourself together, because things are happening. We've finally located Lilly and her mother. We need you and your skills."

"You need mine too." The voice, a mere whisper of her usual presence, had Franklin and Jonah swinging around to stare at Senna. "You woke me."

His hand, the one that reached and cupped her cheek, was unsteady. "I'm sorry, Senna. Jonah was just—"

"We've found them. But you're going to be on medical leave for some time, Senna, so I'll take Franklin and we'll discuss it—"

"No. I can assist Maylin. I'll stay quiet, but I need to be useful. I can't stand being trussed up here and letting you all have the fun." Her voice regained some of its usual force, and he couldn't contain the joy that all but burst from his chest.

"Well, that would have to depend on what Michael has to say."

"I'm not planning on waiting around for him to make up his mind. As soon as I've got the strength to get out of this bed, I'm—"

"You're what?" Michael leaned against the doorjamb, a laconic smile on his face. "You've got a few more days trussed up, I think was the term you used? Then if—and that's a very big if—I'm sure you're up to it, your work status will be carefully monitored. I've worked hard to get you to this point, and you're not going to make me look bad." Michael advanced into the room, displacing Jonah who muttered and stepped into the hall. "You too, Franklin. Wait outside while I take a look at my patient."

"I can stay—"

"Go," they both ordered in unison, and he stepped out, leaving them to it. The curtain around the bed closed with a metallic *zshhh*.

"That's a pretty determined woman you've got there. Sure you can handle her?"

Franklin nodded at Jonah's prodding. "I couldn't think of anyone else I want to be with more."

Jonah clasped him on the shoulder hard enough that his teeth rattled. "Then welcome to the club," he said before he walked off.

Franklin waited, time passing slowly as he leaned against the wall then pushed away as Michael slid the curtaining back. "Amazing woman there. But it will take time and rest. And speaking of rest, she's asleep. Go get some of your own and come see me in the morning when I have a better idea of when she should be released."

Senna swung her legs over the side of the bed. "So, when are you planning to let me out, doc?"

Michael, the cybe-enhanced doctor and close friend of Franklin, smiled. "Maybe tomorrow. Your temp is down, and I can see the healing in your side, which is looking healthy. You're very lucky though, because it wouldn't have had to be much closer and it would have hit your liver. If that had happened..." Michael spread his hands, and she realized how close she'd come to death.

That sobered her. "Who found me?"

"Does it matter?"

She rubbed a hand over her forehead. "I guess not. So, can I help Maylin once I'm released?"

"Yeah. On the proviso you rest. You'll be in her care during the day, and when she tells you to stop, that's what you do, otherwise you're back here. And I'm releasing you into Franklin's care."

Senna couldn't control her scowl.

"You don't want to be in his care?"

Tread carefully, Senna. "It's not that I don't want to, doc, but he's got enough things on his plate. I'm a distraction and I can't do that."

Michael scowled. "Distraction?"

Dammit, I knew I'd stuff this up. "What I meant is, he's got a dangerous mission coming up. I would prefer to be there with him. But instead I've got babysitters, including him. It's splitting his attention, and he could get—"

"Hurt?" The tension in Michael's face melted a little, and the savage headache she'd been battling released slightly.

"Yes."

Michael bent down. "I think he'd be more concerned if you

weren't in his care. He'd be constantly concerned, then his concentration would be split further. At least this way, you're close by until he heads out, then with Maylin. And when he's away, you're welcome to stay with us. Clarissa would probably like some female company about now."

"Uh, sure. Can I think about that?" She picked at the ugly hospital gown. "And when can I have my uniform back?"

He poked at her side, albeit gently, and a ripple of pain and shock surged. "What did you do that for?" Her voice came out like a wheeze.

"When that stops being the case, then a uniform will be acceptable. Nothing that rubs over the wound site, Senna. Now, I've spoken with Daniella, Clarissa, and Erin. They've sent along a range of clothing items for your use," Michael said as he picked up a satchel and waved it before her.

He dropped it beside her, and she peered in. *Dresses.* "Fine. Thanks."

He retreated with, "I'll leave you now. I believe your tea is on the way, and when I see you in the morning, it should be to release you."

CHAPTER 18

Franklin waited as Senna lowered herself into the seat at the briefing. He'd chosen one where she'd be against the wall, thinking that way no one would jostle her injury.

Jonah entered the room, an electronic pad in his hands. "Thank you for coming. Today's briefing is to plan the final push toward reinstating the true government to power and defeating those behind the warrior children. We've received intelligence that leads us to believe Lilly Montaine," he said as her image flashed onto a screen behind Jonah, "is holed up in a cabin in Forsythia, located in the Gerstaldt Ranges. I have reason to believe one of the others in attendance is in fact Vandra Montaine, wife of the late senator. However, the difficulty in proving her identity is that we believe she may not look like, or in fact be, herself any longer."

The ripple of disbelief in the room was a tangible thing. It took everything Franklin had not to jump up and explain how he knew this could, in fact, be true.

"After the attack on the World Bank, we took into custody a person we believed to be Carlos Phenja. That was when we became aware of another series of Dr. Jeremy Colvert's experimentations. He'd been undertaking *brain transplantation*, among other forbidden therapies."

Indrawn breaths and mutters filled the room, the tension palpable.

"His actions are a Level 5 Breach of the Transplantation Ruling and a Code 5 Breach of the Medical Policies Act. We brought the person we thought was Phenja in and discovered it was Larossa in a different body. Needless to say, before we could act, the Larossa-Phenja individual committed suicide. What we do know is the transplantation act itself leads to a chemical imbalance and forces the recipient to become subject to increased chemical imbalances of the brain. Where a negative brain function existed before, it seems to exacerbate the issues. We believe Vandra Montaine exhibits the same status and behaviors."

You could hear a pin drop, the room silent as everyone waited for the next piece of information.

Jonah continued. "Maylin has been working day and night with her team, triangulating the information we have concerning the death of Vandra Montaine, and attempting to link it to those closest to Lilly Montaine now. There are two suspects. First, we have Elmira Sandhurst, one of Lilly's peers, who we know was fatally injured in a car accident just prior to Vandra's death nearly two years ago. She is, in fact, our top contender. There is also Corleone Montarucci." Two more images flashed onto the screen. "Montarucci was a bodyguard to the Montaine family until his disappearance two years ago. There is talk that he was shipped off for a while to cool speculation of a relationship between him and Lilly Montaine. I don't believe he's key, however, both of these individuals are dangerous. Elmira was a decorated shooter of note in the pistol world. Montarucci is listed as a bodyguard but think more of a tame assassin and we have a better idea of him. Dangerous both in terms of his hand-to-hand skills and use of various weapons. We believe he was, and continues to be, in a romantic relationship with Montaine."

Jonah stopped, waited for a moment, hands gripping the podium, and Franklin noted the white of his knuckles. The strain of the situation was telling on his friend, with the first flash of white at his temples, something Franklin hadn't noticed before, and a series of fine lines on the man's forehead and around his eyes.

"Vandra herself was a key strategist for the combat arm of the local militia before she married Senator Montaine after meeting on the range. She is believed to have kept her association, although it was never openly advertised. She was his chief aide in the early days of his campaign. Even though they married and she settled into parenthood, she's still considered a dangerous woman. Rated at level 6 on the Pistol World Champion range at the time of her death, she was and still is likely to be more than competent with sidearms."

In the back row, one of the majors stood. "Sir, given what we know then, how do you plan to—"

Jonah harrumphed, cutting the question short. "That's where you boys come into play. I need a diversion. Something that will keep them focused away from the team we plan to drop into the mountains. We don't know what weaponry or even tools they have to hand. All we know is if they get wind of our assault beforehand, then we've already lost."

Maylin stepped up. "My team and I have been working on plans and contingencies for this kind of situation. We've created a set of short-range communication devices with blockers that will interrupt their external broadcasting capabilities." The little Asian woman held up an earbud device. "This is a powerful tool in ensuring the stealth of our people, and the self-contained battery pack should keep it working for up to seventy-two hours, however, if we lose more than say thirty percent of the overall number, the efficacy of our unit is compromised. We are encoding them to the genetics of the wearer, which means if they lay their hands on a unit, they won't be able to hook into the system."

Jonah thanked her then regained his position at the front of the room.

"I've worked with General Dewan to create a plan, allowing us to access the airways over the mountains. We are sending in a range of decoy planes followed by a Jump-Star team. The teams chosen for the Jump-Star are our best people, and will receive training over the next forty-eight hours. The aim is to prepare them for the mission, the use of the comm devices, and apprise them of the layout of the buildings as much as we've been able to ascertain through accessing known building regs. While those joining the Jump-Star are en route, we are sending teams of combat-ready soldiers into position at the foothills." The screen behind Jonah flashed back into life, and he turned, tapping the map to highlight the locations of the teams. "They will create the diversion and will bring the cabin into, we hope, lockdown. The teams are being pulled together today."

When Jonah's gaze settled on Franklin, he knew he would be a member of the Jump-Star.

"Everyone will be given the opportunity for either a final meeting with family face-to-face or to prepare themselves. This is not an easy battle. We don't know how many warrior children might be there, as we've not been able to ascertain if there's a bunker. Reinforcements are, at this time, arriving at the naval base as we meet from other localities and continents. This is our last and best chance to counter the threat. Let me be frank, our munitions are running low, as are basic foodstuffs. We're being starved out, and this is our last chance. They cannot win. We cannot allow it."

Silence dropped over the room. The information wasn't new, but it highlighted their dire situation. Most of the air traffic had ceased due to the attacks from missiles launched from within the towns, the gas pipelines necessary to power the craft cut off since the launch of the colony ship, and only the naval fleet left, and that too was now feeling the effects of starvation.

"Each of you will be given information concerning your assignments. Ladies and gentlemen, we must make this work. This is the future of humanity, and it lies in your hands."

They rose, thunderous applause crashing through the room until it died away. Jonah sat back down, and Senna squirrelled her hand into his.

"So this is it," she said.

He nodded and turned to face her. "Senna, I have to tell you something. I... I've been a coward and—"

"Yo, Franklin!" Fawcett limped over and settled beside him. "I'm hoping they'll include me, even with this." He indicated to his injured leg.

Franklin cursed his bad luck, wishing everyone except Senna would melt away and let him tell her what he felt.

"I'm sure there'll be a role. Look, can we discuss this later, Fawcett?"

The man's eyes widened. "Oh, of course."

Franklin waited until Fawcett walked away before grabbing both of Senna's hands. "I need to tell you—"

"Franklin, your file. Jonah wants to talk with you." Daniella's aide, Kallee, pushed the folder at him. "I think *now* would be the operative term. Senna, how're you feeling?"

Franklin's frustration pummeled him. "Yeah, sure."

I'll have to make a point to track her down. Later. Then we can talk.

⁓⊰⊱⁓

The teams assembled on the parade grounds. A minister rushed in from the naval base appeared harried as he completed the blessing.

Senna wondered how the preacher felt about blessing units that were about to capture those behind the warrior children movement. Then reality settled, a heavy burden of knowledge, aware that likely most of the children themselves would be incarcerated for the remainder of their lives if they were unable to be rehabilitated.

Hundreds of men and women were heading into what was probably going to be the fight of their lives. "I should be there." It didn't help that Erin, Daniella, and Clarissa crowded around her in solidarity.

The parade ended, and the troops dispersed. Over the last forty hours she'd barely seen Franklin, and with his departure imminent, she wanted some time alone. She marched forward after excusing herself from the women and was halfway across the parade ground when Maylin hailed her. "We've got a problem, and I need your expertise."

The words stopped her in her tracks. "I..." She glanced in his direction and pain speared her. "Yeah, on my way."

Across the grounds Franklin's gaze collided with hers before she turned back in the direction of the building. She moved as quickly as she could, her side still aching, so that by the time she arrived in the basement Maylin had set up as her bunker, it was rather more than a physical discomfort.

Maylin hunched over a unit, her face screwed up with frustration. "Good. One of the scanners is detecting a heat zone. You're the arson specialist. Tell me what you think it is."

On a sigh, Senna dropped into the seat before the scanner. Her eyes moved back and forth, looking for telltale signs she'd learned of during her arson training. Various heat spots showed on the monitor, yet it was one at the back, an almost black mass that wavered.

Senna leaned in closer. "Can you pull a satellite feed for me? I need better vision." She'd seen something like this before, during her training, but pinpointing the source from her memory wasn't an easy task.

"This one, right?" Maylin checked as she tugged the keyboard over so it settled in front of her, and fingers flying, she input commands. Suddenly, the view changed. Arrowed down to the location, then slowly, the image grew.

"Oh my God! They're bodies. Maylin, get Jonah for me. He needs to see this. And how do I make this bigger?" She grabbed the mouse and rolled it, swore when the screen became smaller, then reversed direction. She breathed deeply as it enlarged.

Now she could clearly see a group of people gathered around the fire, not well enough to pick out their features, but there was a mix of men and women. And children. *Warrior children.*

Those burning, and the outlines were clear enough, were obviously dead, but what reason could they have? Unless they were opposing forces.

Footsteps echoed, and Jonah hurried to her side. "Maylin said you'd found something disturbing I needed to see."

"Do you have anyone up there? Informants or civilians?"

"There were families from what I can make out..." His face blanked. "You think they did this to get rid of anyone who—"

"Any threats. I do. I can't say how many, but possibly ten or more. Jonah, I need to get up there. Identify them and—"

"No. I need you here."

"Jonah, I couldn't even manipulate the screen properly. Bed me down with the diversionary forces. When it's clear, I can do what I'm trained for. I'll stay out of the way, but this? What they've done here is cold. It's considered and planned. People who just went about their day-to-day lives. Not hurting anyone, probably contributing citizens. They deserve to be known and remembered and the crimes against them brought to light. You talk about winning the war of minds and hearts? This! This is where we start." Fury dripped in her every word.

He was wavering, she could feel it in the air. "Let me go, Jonah. I'll be useful after the battle. I'll even go to ground until it's over and feed back intel."

"I... Okay." The agreement came through clenched teeth. He pointed at her, his face tight. "But you follow any direction given by the team leader, and we don't tell Franklin."

She bit her lip at that, then nodded her agreement. Keeping this kind of information from him wasn't something she felt comfortable with. "Okay. And just to keep everyone happy, I'll grab a ballistic skinsuit."

He grunted his agreement before turning on his heel and leaving the room.

"Are you sure this is a great idea?" Maylin asked.

"No, not really, but we need accurate information. Stuff I can do. Plus, I'm on the ground as a resource for scanning for explosives. It's not like I'm untrained."

"Just injured," Maylin returned.

here's she gone? Franklin saw Senna just a minute ago, across the parade ground, but now she'd disappeared. He only had hours before they shipped out. The urgency grabbed him by the scruff of the neck and shook him hard.

He stalked across the asphalt, heading toward Erin, Daniella, and Clarissa, who waited for him. "Senna?"

"Maylin needed her for a moment. But before you go, we've got something for you. Or at least organized," said Clarissa, a small smile on her face.

"What?"

"It's a surprise, but if you follow me, I think you'll like it."

The two women smiled as he followed the blonde across the now empty parking lot and onto the roadway. "The cabin at the end is empty. The family that was supposed to be housed there didn't make it. We kept it empty in case of need and…well, Daniella, Erin, and I all agreed that right now you guys need privacy. So, we kinda co-opted it from the housing unit. Only for twenty-four hours, as we can't do anything else, but you know." Clarissa shrugged, and on a whim, he reached out and hugged her.

"Thank you."

She sniffed. "We put some supplies in too. No wine, but some sparkling juice and food." The woman looked over her shoulder, her eyes glowing blue, alerting him she was using her cybernetic abilities. "Michael says he's heading over to Maylin's office. He'll send Senna this way." The blue glare in her eyes faded as she turned back. "Now, I'll leave you alone. She won't be long."

He opened the door, for a moment fantasizing that she was waiting, the war was over, and their future assured.

Could he be a good father and husband? He hadn't had the experience of a positive role model, and yet, he knew instinctively that he could be. The scent of food wafted on the air, threading through his senses along with roses. He closed the door and allowed himself to hope for more.

Franklin settled on laying out the meal, hoping she wouldn't be long. It was only a short while before the door opened, admitting her.

Her face shined as she took in the scene. "You prepared the meal."

"I wanted to surprise you."

Franklin passed her a glass of the bubbling juice, and she smiled. It warmed him all the way to his guts. Her laugh was carefree, and she slid her arm around his waist.

"Isn't this a great surprise? I didn't know anything about it until they had it organized," he said.

Unable to wait any longer, Franklin bent down, sliding his lips over hers, trying to tell her wordlessly of both his passion and his love. He kept it light, because he still had something to say.

"Senna, I tried to tell you more than once. Every time you've either fallen asleep or we've been interrupted. I mean, my timing is pretty bad but..." His stomach jittered. *How the hell do I say it?* "What I'm trying to say is... I love you. You're the most perfect thing, a gift I never expected to get. I want us to have a future together. Tell me you feel the same?"

Nerves danced in his belly as he waited. He looked away, not wanting to push her, but needing her to speak. *Say something. Anything.*

Silence stretched. "Senna?"

She hiccupped, and he glanced at her, saw tears glistening on her cheeks.

"Did I say something wrong?" God knew the blockage in his throat was just about asphyxiating him.

"I..." She sniffed, breathed deeply, took his hand in hers. "I love you too, Franklin. And this is not me."

He laughed at her comment. "No. A watering pot you aren't."

Franklin snatched the drink from her hand, then pulled her close, nestling her against his wildly beating heart, all the while in thankfulness.

"You know, I've been out of the medical center for days and you've barely touched me."

He grinned at her sultry tone. "Because of your injury." He cupped her face, keeping the touches light and playful.

"My injury. Of course. Well, I've been cleared for certain more rigorous activities now. So long as I don't overexert..." Senna fluttered her lids, and laughter rumbled in his chest.

"Then let's not waste that clearance."

The kiss was cataclysmic, burning through Senna's body. Franklin's lips sipped and demanded entry to her mouth. Emotions welled, hunger and passion clashing against her sense of smell, wild musk filling the air as he carefully and slowly stripped the cotton gown from her body.

"Franklin," she hissed as his lips slid down the line of her throat, finding the sensitive spot below her jaw.

His tongue twirled on the spot, and she shivered, nerves dancing madly as moisture and heat pooled, dampening her underwear.

His fingers slid under the straps of her bra, hooking them and gently pulling until they dropped over her shoulders, and her breasts, heavier than before, sagged. Her nipples, sensitive dots of pleasure, scraped against the cups, and she sighed as he dragged them from her body.

"Did I tell you how beautiful you are, Senna?" he murmured against her skin, and her belly quavered.

The need to participate was overwhelming, so she turned in his arms and slid hers around his waist.

"You moved," he complained, and she giggled.

"I want to be involved too, you know." She burrowed her fingers deep, tugging at his shirt until she reached the waistband. She slid her fingertips along the tip of his cock and felt him shiver at her touch. "Like that, do you?"

His hands skimmed the skin of her back. She stepped away, feet unsteady as her mind whirled under the intimate onslaught, and the cool air caressed her skin, nipples puckered into tight buds.

"Take off your shirt, Franklin." Her voice shook with arousal.

Gazes meshed, and he tugged the piece of clothing with slow and steady movements. Her mouth dried as his bronzed flesh was revealed, and she curled her fingers, holding onto the greedy urge to touch and claim just a little longer.

He reached out, sliding a finger over her belly, so the nerves quivered in response. "Franklin?" The word was an invitation as she hooked her thumbs into her panties and slid them down her body.

His gaze narrowed, face hardening with desire.

"Join me?" She turned and crooked her finger, calling him to follow.

Once in the small bedroom, Franklin's hands fumbled on the fastener of his pants. They slipped and he swore, a crest of red tiding his cheeks.

She reached out, and he stepped away, his body vibrating as his eyes glazed. "I won't last if you touch me right now, Senna." He inhaled deeply, head bowed, and she waited, giving him time and space without withdrawing completely. Once more in control, Franklin's fingers released the clasp of his pants, and they fell to the floor with a whisper, his boxers stark white against the bronzed skin.

Unable to stop herself, Senna reached, trailing her fingers over the band. "A man in boxers is very sexy. But even better when he's out of them."

His trembling hands framed her face, and he looked deeply into her eyes, as if searching her soul. "So long as I'm the only man wearing boxers for you, or not."

"Only you," she agreed. Senna slid his underwear over his hips, past the jutting length of his erection, then forgot them as they came together again, skin against skin.

She moaned as her peaked nipples brushed his chest, shattered what was left of their combined control, and the kiss that followed was ravenous. Lips moving and teeth scraping with the urgency.

His hands cupped her breasts, flicked at the nubs as she cried out, back arching. "Franklin." The word telegraphed her hunger.

They moved—him directing Senna to the bed—until the metal

rubbed behind the back of her legs, sending her down with a thud, and he followed, his body mashed against hers.

"I could eat you up," he growled, lips sliding against hers, hips grinding as her legs opened, bracketing his waist and pulling him closer to her burning heat.

Franklin's cock nudged at the lips of her sex, sliding with in without resistance, her arousal coating him. "Please," she entreated, hands curved over his shoulders, needing him closer. Tugging at him so he'd follow her urgent demands.

"I want more than a quick release, Senna. I want everything. I want to grow old with you." The timbre of his words dragged her momentarily from the fog of passion. In his eyes Senna read both promise and hope.

It took seconds for her brain to form a response. "Good to hear. I want that too, but later. Now, I want you," she rasped. Flexing her legs, Senna pulled him closer, urged him to fill her, and when he did, the sensation of fullness completed her, while ratcheting that hot coil of hunger tighter.

She dropped once more into the well of pleasure, where sounds and scents fed the need in her soul. Musk filled the air along with their cries and moans. In this world, only the two of them in that moment existed.

Senna slid her fingers over miles of hot flesh, then gripped his ass, her nails biting into his firm skin as she urged him on. Her thighs flexed, and they slid and rocked together in the most ancient of rhythms. Every sound enhancing the intimacy as they sought the orgasm that lay just beyond them both.

His mouth, hot and urgent, settled over her breast as stars shattered beneath her closed eyelids. "Fra... Franklin!" She arched, back off the bed as she tangled her fingers in his hair and pulled tight.

"Senna, come for me," he chanted, moving faster and harder and wilder until she couldn't tell where the next wave would crash over her.

One final move and she splintered.

Down.

Deep.

Somewhere far away he called, emptied himself deep within her body, and hot tears scorched her cheeks.

"I love you, Franklin," she whispered.

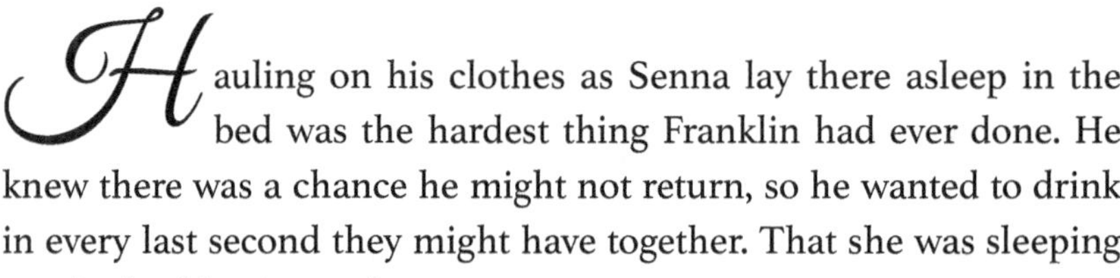

*H*auling on his clothes as Senna lay there asleep in the bed was the hardest thing Franklin had ever done. He knew there was a chance he might not return, so he wanted to drink in every last second they might have together. That she was sleeping was both a blessing and a curse.

"I love you, Senna."

On the pillow beside her, he dropped a small case, the one he'd bartered for after learning she was still alive. He'd wanted to give it to her last night, but at the time it felt cruel. Now, in the light of day, he rethought his decision to propose this way. The hastily scrawled message inside told her what he should have said last night.

With a final glance, he carefully pulled the sheet over her nude body, then turned and left the cabin. As the door clicked shut, he was sure he'd left the best of himself behind with the woman he loved.

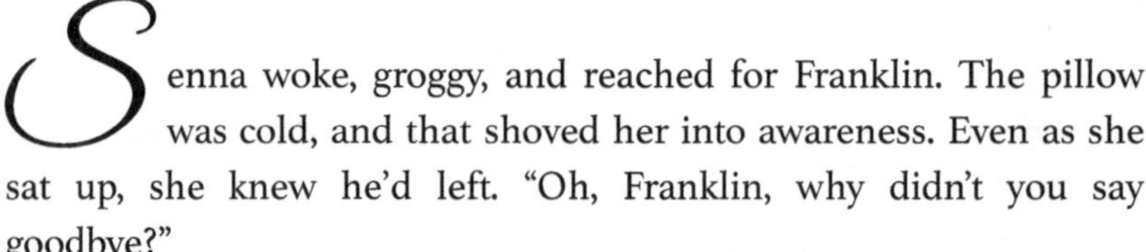

*S*enna woke, groggy, and reached for Franklin. The pillow was cold, and that shoved her into awareness. Even as she sat up, she knew he'd left. "Oh, Franklin, why didn't you say goodbye?"

The small blue box he'd laid on her pillow cracked the shell around her heart. Tears dribbled as she reached for the box, and inside lay a ring, a tiny diamond winking at her through her tears. Inside the box was a rolled piece of paper. Her fingers shook as she plucked it out and unrolled it.

Senna,

I wanted to ask last night, but I was a coward.
Marry me.
Wear this ring as a promise I'll return if I can. If not, wear it in my memory.
With all my love forever.
Franklin

A sob erupted, followed by another, and she gave in to the fear that swallowed her. The weeping gave way to hope. "You'll come back to me, Franklin, even if I have to hunt you down."

The ring, slender and intricate, didn't weigh much, until she slipped it on. Now the promise contained in this small gift carried the weight of her hope and love. It twinkled in the light, and she stared at it. The bright jewel picking up the stray sunrays that slid through the curtains.

With a tiny sigh, she rose, dressed with efficiency, and prepared for the day.

Senna's hand had just touched the handle of the door when three knocks sounded. "Come in."

Jonah entered, the skinsuit they had agreed she would wear in his arms. "They're rolling out in fifteen. You'll be in the final wagon, and Franklin's already on his way to the plane. You need to be fast. I'll wait for you outside with your bag of tricks."

"Jonah? I know it feels wrong to keep it from him, but *thank you.*"

His nod was curt until his gaze caught sight of the ring. He glanced up, his eyes wide. "Franklin will kill me if anything happens to you, so no chances, understand?"

She nodded, at a loss for words because that damned lump, the one she'd thought had melted away, returned to her throat. "I'll be quick."

Shutting the door, Senna shucked off the dress and slid into the skinsuit, then sighed, looking at her bare feet.

She opened the door again, and Jonah held out socks and boots, which she gratefully accepted. "How long do you think it will take to reach the mountains?"

He shrugged as she tugged on the shoes, thankful he'd had someone retrieve her own worn-in favorites. "Ten, maybe twelve hours. Franklin's team will make an initial stop at a closer abandoned base. I had men clear it so they're closer and can move quickly. They'll have a quick refresher course, then be airborne tonight, ready for the drop."

Standing, Senna followed him out of the cabin, but as she closed the door, she turned, hoping that one day she and Franklin would return to it. She shook her head at the whimsical notion that it was a tangible reminder of what lay between them, as much as the tiny ring on her finger.

"You'll need to remove the ring." Jonah spoke quietly, and she wanted to argue, but of course, he was right.

"I don't want to leave it behind."

He reached up and unfastened a chain surrounding his neck. "Daniella gave me this. Use it, but give it back when you're done," he said gruffly, handing the gold links to her.

"Oh, Jonah, I can't."

He stopped abruptly, and she cannoned into him. "He's my best friend, Senna. My brother in every way that counts. Wear the ring on it."

Tears stung her eyes, and she nodded. "Okay. I'll look after it."

With a quick motion, she slid the ring from her finger, feeling the loss immediately, and popped it onto the chain. It slid over her head, and she dropped it out of sight under the neck of her suit, close to her heart.

"Good. Now get on that truck." Jonah shoved the rifle slung over his shoulder at her and her bag into her hands. "Be safe. Hunt well."

Without any more to say, she hurried forward, climbed into the truck, and settled into the last spot, waiting for the roll call.

The tailgate was fastened, the flaps over the back of the truck closed as the engine began with a rumble, then it lumbered forward, heading for the fight.

CHAPTER 19

The air-transport rumbled through the night, the rear door now wide open, and the wind made it hard to hear. One by one, those who were jumping stood, fastened themselves to the safety line, and moved forward, the sack on their back containing the chute that would carry them safely to the ground.

Franklin shuffled forward, constantly replaying the instructions in his head. *Attain a stable position. Arms slightly ahead, back arched and head up. Pull the lever with the right arm, left across the body. Legs together and hold chin down. Aim for a feet first landing with knees bent to absorb shock.*

Finally, he was there, staring into the abyss. His clip released, and he was falling, the air rushing past him as he worked through the steps. The chute deployed with a thud, but his fall slowed and he had time to prepare.

It was over in moments, his feet once more connecting with the earth, and he thanked the deities for their care.

He stripped out of the chute, rolled it up, and looked for a safe stash point.

Others landed nearby, and he trudged to the pre-assigned meeting point, the whole time silence his friend. Glancing at his watch, he noted they were slightly behind schedule. *More time for the diversion to set in.*

The mountainous terrain featured a range of flat plains, and that was where they had come down, within a mile of the meeting point, and once more he gave thanks. As the group came together, he tugged a carefully shielded torch from his pack and the map, and as the men gathered, they settled under a tree, canteens passed around and some dry biscuits consumed.

"Right, the diversionary operation should be starting soon. We need to get into position, wait for the flares to tell us they're ready for us to move." He'd already grouped the men by skillsets and reminded them of the coordinates of their starting points. "Stealth is of the utmost importance. Even when the diversion begins, we can't be sure they won't have a body of children standing by just in case, hidden in some bunker. We know their strategic planning is poor, but for my money, I'd expect their best to be on standby, and of course those directing the actions, protecting their queen."

"They would have seen the trucks though. Won't that tip them off?"

Franklin had thought long and hard about that. "Yeah, but they're only aware that those troops were deployed. Unless they caught wind of the planes, our position here should be safe. But we have to move quickly and quietly. Now, the earbuds you were issued are new. They've got a scrambler built in and can pick up any sound, no matter how quiet. Fit them, then get moving."

He stood and waited as the teams headed off, melding into the night. With him were Sevres, Fairburn, David, and Erin. *All capable and highly trained.* Their chances of survival were better than most, but it was no foregone conclusion.

"Stay together and focused. We don't know what we're going into." With those words, Franklin started the final march to battle.

*B*y the time the truck stopped, Senna felt battered and bruised. *I'd forgotten what it's like to be in the back of one of these trucks!*

The back opened, and she jumped out and moved to the side. *Just like old times.* Except this time she wasn't supposed to be in the thick of things. Jonah's admonition played in her mind, and she looked about, seeking cover, a place to hunker down during the worst of the fighting.

She was there for one purpose only. To find out who those murdered were and to ensure they wouldn't be forgotten. But she wasn't a fool. If the children worked out that she, or anyone else opposing them for that matter, was there, they'd have no qualms in killing her.

The team leader trotted over. "You're aware you are not to participate in any action?"

Senna nodded, aware of the restrictions Jonah had placed on her. "Yes, I'm to look for cover."

"Yes, however, we did wonder if you'd be able to take the military vid-processer with you. He's also to remain out of the field of battle, but to be honest, he's a dead weight. If I have to appoint someone to babysit him—"

"That's fine, send him to me." Senna watched as some of the tension eased from the man's face.

"Good. We were about to look around and determine a sheltering locality—"

"Leave that with me, sir. I'll find somewhere to hunker down." If Senna were honest, it felt better to have something, a responsibility, during this time. She felt that there was now a justifiable reason for her to be there.

The man left and returned a few minutes later. The tall, thin man with him was clearly out of place, the uniform he wore fitting his legs but pouching at his waist. "Devonham Illes at your service."

Fish out of water here, Senna. "Nice to meet you. Now come with me, and we'll find somewhere to shelter."

"I do need to be near the battle."

Senna rolled her eyes at the man's tone. "I'll do my best, but this is not an ordinary situation, Devonham." She gripped his sleeve, tugged hard as he looked away over the field before them. "We also don't have a lot of time, so come on."

She trudged through the treeline, searching for roots they could bury themselves in yet keep an eye on the action.

Emotions ran high, the darkness settling as she scooped away some dirt with her foot and aimed the torch on her belt into the dark recess below. "This should do."

"But..."

She glanced at the man to her side, already regretting accepting this task. "It's that or you get back on that truck and get out of here."

"But the public and their right to know—"

"Your problem, not mine. I was told to keep you safe, and that's what I'm doing. Now get in there and be quiet."

Devonham muttered about dirt in his lenses and cleanliness as she followed him down.

Senna simply tugged off her pack and pulled out some camouflage netting, adjusted it, and scowled. "I'm going out to find leaves and light branches to drape over the net. Stay here and be quiet." She slid up and out, moving quickly before she dropped down once again.

"What about if I need to..."

She turned to him. "You hold it," she growled, and he blinked; a pair of white eyes in the dark. Quickly, she found what was required and set about staging their hiding place.

"My camera?"

With a sigh, she took it, and rearranged the netting so it draped without giving away their location. "There."

A boom echoed. The ground shook.

"It's started," she said. "Now be quiet, no matter what you hear or see."

Franklin hunkered down, heat-seeking binocs to his face as he scanned. "I'm reading multiple life forms in this building. If the specs we secured are correct, this is where our main targets will be holed up." He turned his attention to the next building and swore. "At least thirty if I'm reading correctly in the building to the left. None in the right... Hang on a couple, but they appear to be asleep. Could be our guards are a mixture of daytime and night variety. Fan out and check the grounds. I need intel on any patrols."

Though he was barely whispering he knew all the men had heard his commands, and he waited patiently.

How on earth did they do this before the gadgetry we have now?

The first blip came as the thought melted. "I've got a team, maybe ten or twelve on the far edge and a platoon or more making their way down the mountain. They've taken the bait."

Sevres nodded with quick moves, and his excitement speared Franklin. That was one group they'd need to be assured were long gone before they began their attack. The last thing him and his small band could cope with was in influx.

But still, he needed more information. A clear picture of what they faced so they could tailor their attack for the best outcome. "Fairburn?"

"I'm reading nil life forms in the rear cabin near the pit. I'd say, given the size of it though, it's where the majority were camped. The smell is pretty rank here, Franklin."

It would be, given what we've seen on the feed.

One by one, the other team members responded in kind. No other warriors in residence. Unless there was a hidden bunker. His scalp itched, warning him to unseen danger. This surely couldn't be their entire force. Yet he also felt a surge of something close to pleasure that thus far things were going as well as could be expected.

"Right, get yourselves back here," Franklin ordered, "but watch for guards and surprises."

His men all knew how to melt into the darkness, were highly trained, but their enemies weren't the usual combat-ready soldier. No, they were kids. Badly in some cases or half-trained and led by people with only some military and strategic training. They couldn't afford to take any of this cheaply because they could and likely would react badly.

Once his men reassembled, he breathed a sigh of relief. When Fairburn opened his mouth to speak, Franklin held up a hand to stop him. If they'd been seen, a posse would be quickly forthcoming.

Franklin waited, listened. Quiet.

He knew the silence meant nothing, but time was slipping away. They had to act now. "Break into three teams, and we move on the buildings."

He gave the signal and they moved away, his group creeping forward toward the buildings, as he heard the booms and crashes from the battle below. The others had engaged the enemy. He just had to hope the diversion worked the way he planned.

His much smaller posse circled the building where only a few lay sleeping within. The door opened silently, and he sent up a prayer of thanks for whoever had oiled the hinges.

They advanced on the sleeping children, and he reached into his small pouch, pulled out a hypo spray, and hit the first child, while the others took care of the two others.

"Fasten them up, then slide them back under their covers. We can't afford to blow our cover if someone checks."

The ties they'd packed slid around wrists and ankles, then they finished off with tape over their mouths.

"Good work," Franklin said.

A sound echoed from outside, and the frantic thud of his heart seemed loud enough that surely whoever was outside would hear it.

"Clear," came a voice, and he and the team scurried under the bunk beds at the back of the room. They'd just hidden when the door cracked open. "All appears fine in bunkroom four."

He waited as the patrolling officer, a youth of perhaps sixteen or so, scanned the room. *Does he suspect something?*

He held his breath until the door shut. Well-trained, they remained still and silent. The oldest trick in the book was to close the door as if they were leaving, then their quarry would think the coast was clear until the watcher slid back into view.

When the door opened again, they were still safe, hiding.

His breath stirred the air under the bed, a sneeze building in his throat as eddies of dust rose.

When the door shut again, he closed his eyes, controlled every impulse, but the sneeze erupted anyway.

He crawled out, signaled to the others do the same, and they crept to the door and peered around.

The guard who'd entered stood at the corner, scanning something on a hand-held unit, and a split-second decision propelled Franklin forward, hypo in hand. The boy dropped before he could raise the alarm.

"Get him into the bunk room." He bent, scooped up the communications unit, and swore upon seeing the details on the screen. *Heightened security—breach expected.*

"They're not onto us yet, but we need to move fast. They're expecting some attempt at a breach and recalling units."

The second team called in, advising that they'd secured the other occupied bunkhouse. Now for the main building.

They moved with speed now, feet churning as they neared the building. Then once against the rough wooden exterior, they stopped and took a moment to catch their breath. He reached once more for the pouch hanging from his side.

"We need to take them alive if we can. Engage masks." The small device in his hands would emit a sleeping gas. The other team members were similarly equipped, re-breathers which they attached firmly.

On the count of three, he smashed the plasglass window nearest and lobbed the small ball inside.

He heard echoes of the same action, watched as wafts of gray smoke emanated.

It would only be a matter of moments, but every precious second counted toward the lives and deaths on the battlefield.

Franklin curled his hands into a fist, counted down in his head, then pushed up, going in the direction of the nearest door.

It crashed open, and he fell as something went *bang* near his location. "They've booby-trapped the building," he yelled, a cacophony of sounds coming from varied directions.

Feet thudded, and he shifted away, rolling and levering up from the floor.

Black-clad legs raced into the room, kids wearing masks. "They expected something like this."

Not well thought out, Franklin!

Still, they were better trained. He moved forward, ready to counter their attack, as a pair of black legs caught his attention from the side. He feinted, dropped for the deck, and swept out with his leg.

An *oomph* sounded, and he tore off the mask of the first child. Enough of the sleeping gas remained that it would do the job. Two more came at him, he missed a jab to the ribs from the first and returned a kick to the knee. The kid screamed and went down.

His fingers scrabbled for the breather as the third charged. Eyes glinting in the smoky haze, he reached and a *pop* sounded.

A splatter of blood and pain radiated from his shoulder.

In the doorway, a woman stood, laser pistol in hand. "You won't defeat us."

CHAPTER 20

Senna wasn't sure what made her uneasy at first. They were well-hidden, weren't they? The battle was far enough away... Until the sound of vehicles and incendiary devices echoed.

"We have to get out of here," she screamed at Devonham, who sat stock-still, just as he had since the beginning of the battle.

"But... But they'll *kill* us!"

His wheezing words didn't stop as Senna frantically tugged at the netting over the top of them. "They'll kill us anyway. Hear those fizzing noises? They're incendiary devices. They'll burn anything in their path."

The wild thud of her heart almost drowned out the screams she heard, but there was no way she'd bow to the terror ripping at her brain.

She reached down and tugged the man by the arm. "Ever climbed a tree before? Or a rock wall?"

He blinked at her. "What?"

"We're going to head into the forest. There's a sheer rock wall, but if we can make it up one of the trees, we'll be on a ledge. There're usually caves in these types of mountainous regions. We get in, hide."

He shook. "But I don't run."

With a growl, she reached for the man, hoisted up the camera, and screamed, "You do now."

He was a weight, every step twice as hard because he was either unfit or unwilling to run. But he was also her responsibility, and she took that seriously.

"Come on," she cajoled, and hissed when he tripped and fell.

"Go on without me," he cried, a piteous lump at her feet.

"If only," she muttered, tugging Devonham up again as the sound of wheels squeaked nearer. "We don't have time for this. Now move!" Senna dug deep, found every ounce of fury and leadership and infused it into the words, and this time, without a sound, he followed her command.

They reached the sheer rockface.

"How... You expect me to climb that?"

"Yes. Now climb this tree here. Get up!"

"I'm... I'm afraid of heights," he whined, and she growled.

Give me strength! "Move it, otherwise we're dead."

He blinked, and she shoved him, waited as he gripped the trunk, then she gave him a push. Finally satisfied he'd reached a high enough branch, she headed up behind him. At the top, she scanned and started to shove her weight back and forth so the tree swayed.

"What... *What are you doing*?"

One more pass and she gripped a boulder. "Climb over quickly."

He did, moaning and crying the whole time, and she wanted to hit him, anything to stop the noise. "Hold my hand and pull me, otherwise I won't make it."

Indeed, the tree would fling her back, either into the next one or down to the ground. She took a moment to prepare, exhaled, and pushed off, muscles screaming with exhaustion. Even as she moved, so did the tree, in the opposite direction, and she flung herself. He grabbed both arms and tugged. Feet dangling against the rockface, she fought for and found purchase, slid around the boulder and onto the ledge.

Gasping for breath, Senna wondered how the hell they would survive this hellish situation. Fires licked at the forest, smoke clogging, and now for the first time, she could see the reason for the sound of a vehicle. The all-terrain vehicles they'd come here in had been taken by warrior kids and they'd mowed down trees.

Probably looking for those getting away. Senna tugged Devonham down behind the boulder, finger on her mouth, indicating he needed to be silent.

He nodded, perspiration trickling down his face, his eyes wide open. She noted the bellowing of his chest and hoped she wouldn't need to deal with a cardiac issue.

Peering around the side, she cautiously watched the warrior kids' actions. They clambered out. Argued, hands flying before throwing something at the vehicle, then they ran, laughter filling the air, and she smelled the smoke.

"Damn. Stay down, Devonham!"

The boom was followed by raining metal. She covered him with her body, more than aware that anything else would telegraph their position if the kids had remained nearby.

They coughed, and she checked, sighing when she realizing they were alone. She stood, her body protesting the aches as they pushed aside the rubble from the now smoking hulk.

"Come on. I need to get you inside and safe, then get out there. They may need my skills."

He babbled, but she ignored him. Senna knew things were pretty dire, and even though she was only one person, her skills in the field would assist.

The first cavern she found was shallow, so she discounted it, but the second appeared to be just what she was looking for.

A quick scan satisfied her, and she pressed a small laser pistol into his hands. "If it's not me, shoot. I don't care who it is. Here's some rations." She shoved the packet into his hands. "I'll be back."

Now she ran, the ache in her side reminding her she wasn't yet in optimal condition as he cried, "Don't leave me alone here!"

The man-made ledge continued for some distance, and she followed it, aware that these areas had been mined in the past for the minerals contained in the rock. When she reached the end, Senna stilled and looked out. The trees thinned, and for the first time, she could see the carnage.

Knots of fighting remained, and Senna dropped herself down, sliding on the shale rock until she reached the base. A small laser pistol in hand, she advanced, looking for enemy combatants. She'd nearly cleared the forest when two ran into view. One saw her, gave a warning shout, and headed toward her. She set the pistol to stun and fired. It found its mark, and the child fell, but the other, quick as a snake, ran and tackled Senna.

She went down, assuming a defensive position.

A fist found its way to her stomach, and purely on instinct, Senna reacted, blocked the second blow, then aimed a short punch at the child's face. Blood spurted, and the kid reared back. Her pistol lost in the tussle, she reached for her pocket and palmed a hypo. As the kid made to hit her again, she jabbed it hard against the kid's neck. He slumped and she pushed away, her chest heaving as her lungs screamed for oxygen after the exertion.

"I'm getting too old for this," she muttered and stood, looked down, and found her pistol.

With efficient moves, she tied up the kids to the nearest tree, making sure they were secure, then padded off.

Senna headed for the field when the boom hit, and she looked up. Her mouth hung open and her heart stopped its rhythm. On the mountain above, a plume of smoke and debris rained down.

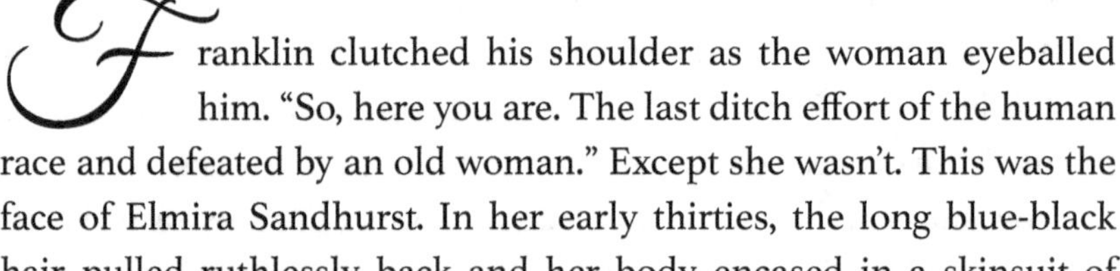

Franklin clutched his shoulder as the woman eyeballed him. "So, here you are. The last ditch effort of the human race and defeated by an old woman." Except she wasn't. This was the face of Elmira Sandhurst. In her early thirties, the long blue-black hair pulled ruthlessly back and her body encased in a skinsuit of what he assumed was ballistic material.

"Mrs. Montaine, I presume."

She smiled a tight grin. "Yes and no. But since it's all over, my warriors have overtaken the field, it's all a bit late. So, I can take some time, share my greatness with you before you meet your end."

The lack of concern on the woman's part was unnerving. After all, she might have him controlled but his people were the best. He had to not only believe they'd carry the day but do it quickly.

So, he'd let her talk, and he'd capture it all, relay it back to base.

"Of course, I had hoped Jonah would come himself. And David. Such a nice boy growing up, shame he and his siblings chose the wrong side. Daniella would have been an amazing assist to our side, but there you go." She spoke with light tones, waving one hand in the air. "But you? You're simply a grunt. One I can use. My warriors need training and I'm sure you'd do an admirable job. We just need to harvest your knowledge from your mind."

His skin crawled as he realized exactly what she was alluding to.

"Oh yes, we've got that technology, thanks to the work of Dr. Jeremy Colvert and his students. They made such strides while conducting their experiments. Shame we lost the girl and she somehow broke the connection. But these later generation children, they have been rewarded. We learned a lot from his experiments."

He tried to put two and two together. "You mean they're connected?"

"What? Oh yes, I only need to give the command now to the central warrior, but don't worry about that. They're all here with me. My children. A much better way to create life than giving birth."

At that he scanned the room with his gaze. *Where is Lilly?*

"Looking for my daughter? Don't worry about her. She's only one of many and flawed. But we will rebuild her, just as we did with Clarissa. She'll make an excellent warrior one day."

Fear bloomed. "Here? You're working on her now?

The woman grinned, lips spread wide like scarlet slashes. "Of course. I've been working on building this facility ever since Jeremy was taken prisoner by your lot. Can't lose my momentum, now can I?"

The cramping in his stomach grew. They had to stop the mad

woman because if she created another cybe, one without the restrictions of empathy no one ever would be safe.

Franklin knew, without a doubt though, there was no humanity in this woman to appeal to. Instead he rose, unsteady and weak from blood loss. His mind now a fuzzy mess. "You can't do this."

The glint of mirth burned away as madness shined in her gaze. "Who's going to stop me? You?" Her laugh grated on him, and he used the strident sound to hold onto consciousness. *One hypo left.* Franklin sucked in an unsteady breath and pounced.

She went down, arms and legs flying.

They scrabbled together and he aimed for her arm, but the hypo bounced off. He hissed as she dug her nails into the injury.

Franklin tucked his chin to his chest and flashed up, catching her bony jaw. She flew back, head striking the doorjamb with a thud.

He panted, found the hypo and injected her anyway. They needed her secured.

Franklin's fingers slipped, blood dripping down her arm as he utilized the ties and bound her securely. The tape he slipped across her mouth then without a moment to lose, pressed his comm. "Find the operating theatre. They're undertaking cybe-therapy on Lilly. We have to stop them before the implants are completed."

Feet flew, men acknowledged. Dimly he heard the sound of combat and slipped through the doorway, then stilled.

His men had done their work. Teams of children lay supine on the floor, every one secured and Erin and David trained pistols on them.

Franklin smiled, the first tight grin to pass his mouth since the mission began. "Well done. I've got Mrs. Montaine in the next room. I'll bring her in."

David nodded, and he marched back in and dragged her into the room, dumped her in the corner. "Watch her. She's not quite right in the head."

"The others?"

"They've spread out, mostly upstairs looking. They're reporting nothing unusual." He snarled, knowing there had to be more.

Now Franklin followed the corridor, opening the doors as he went. At the far end he entered a room, frowned when he noted it went nowhere and there were no windows.

"Unusual," he muttered and began poking and prodding at the walls.

He tried pushing at the notches on the wooden walls, pressing the leaves of ornately carves leaves. A bookcase, lined floor to ceiling beckoned next and he tugged on every book and hissed when a click sounded. The bookcase pivoted and he grinned. "Follow the hall to the end room. Secret door hidden in a bookcase."

"Inventive," responded David, and Franklin grinned at the dry observation.

The man joined him moments later and he pulled the door open to reveal an ante-room of stark white and the door ahead featured a small round plasglass window. He peered inside and almost threw up.

Surgeons surrounded a body, or at least the remains. "They've already begun." He turned and saw David looked as ill as he felt.

"So now what?"

"We contact Jonah and Michael. We don't have the skill and expertise."

"We have to stop them though, otherwise they'll continue while we wait."

David was right. Two more of his men joined them. "Sevres and Fairburn. Go in. Stop the surgery but have them keep her on ice. I don't know what else we do. I'll contact Jonah and Michael. David you stay here, I'll send Erin down to assist you while I make contact. No one else in and only the non-essential medical staff out."

He retreated, to the room beyond and called in to base. "Jonah, we have a problem. They've started surgery on Lilly Montaine. Cybe Therapy."

The man swore. "We need assistance from Michael. He or Windhower will know what needs to be done."

The line blanked for moments then both Dr. Sara Windhower and Michael filled the comm screen. "What step are they at?"

"I'll check." He retraced his footsteps to the theatre and stepped within.

Franklin averted his eyes, not so much because he hadn't seen injuries and death before, but because this was a needless and intrusive operation. One that was both unnecessary and immoral, to his thinking. "I need to know what's been done."

The surgeon simply smiled. "I won't be telling."

Franklin growled at the response and the frustration he felt had his fist balling. He contained himself. "If she dies…"

The surgeon shrugged. "Others will be doing the same. All over the world. The call went out and our people are legion." In his eyes lit the fire of mania and a shiver coursed down Franklin's spine.

"You're mad," he whispered, but the man simply smiled. "No. Driven by the cause."

He reached for a hypo and Franklin pushed his hand away, but not before the hypo discharged against his hand. "What…"

The lights dimmed and he fell, aware of his loss of consciousness. "Call Michael… Tell him…"

Even as he lost awareness the bitter scent of smoke rose.

*S*enna wheezed, her gaze searching for the reason the children simply stopped. Now, they appeared lost, as if someone had flicked a switch. She set about rounding them up, making them sit on the ground before looking for others who could assist with guarding the children.

The soldiers limped and stomped over. "What the hell happened?" demanded one, and she could only shrug. "I don't honestly know. They just gave up and now they seem lost."

A senior officer took over command and she found some with medical training and they started the process of making their way through the wounded. Her triage training wasn't advanced, but she was able to assist those with breaks and the more minor injuries while the others dealt with the life-threatening variety.

The comm in her ear squarked to life. "Senna, the base is clear but we have an issue. What's your location?"

She couldn't help the frown, felt the muscles of her face contracting as she wiped away a bead of sweat. "What? Jonah, what's wrong?"

"Franklin. He's down." Her heart stopped at the words.

"Down? Jonah, what do you mean by—"

"He's been injected with something. Michael's on his way and we'll pick you up at the same time."

Her mouth dried. "I'll be ready." She raced back to the officer in charge. "The historian. He's in a cavern, up the ledge beyond the trees and about a mile or so along. The big cavern. You'll know it. He's armed with a laser pistol and I told him to shoot anyone who wasn't me."

The man stared. "What? You armed a civilian?"

She shrugged. "Not much of a choice really. He's going to need to be collected."

He shook his head. "You go, I don't have man-power."

Senna shrugged. "Jonah is sending a copter for me. I'm needed up there." She pointed to the mountain where plumes of smoke eddied.

She ran back to the appointed location and waited, picking at her nails while her gut implored her to be quick because Franklin needed her.

Minutes later the whomp and thump of a copter echoed, great gusts of wind kicked up by the rotors and she waited until Michael waved her over and bent over hurried in its direction. The door opened and she thrust herself inside.

"Michael—"

Before she could say a word he shook his head. "I don't know, Senna. So just hang on."

They lifted, and the ground spun away as she silently urged greater speed from their transport. Minutes later, they hovered over a building, gray plumes rising into the air and they set down.

"Come with me, we'll find Franklin then you can get about your business." She reached for her satchel then groaned. "Problem?"

"I left it..."

Michael rubbed her shoulder. "We didn't know your status so Jonah sent the standby. The one you had him hold onto."

She felt foolish and yet pleased she'd prepared for the worst. "Okay."

David beckoned them forward. "They hit him with a hypo. The doctor won't say what but it was about that time an alarm tripped and something ignited in the building. We evacuated, but Lilly Montaine..." He shook his head. "We tried."

On the ground lay a shrouded body, red seeped out and she knew immediately. There lay the remains of Lilly Montaine.

Rows of others, she was sure they were breathing, lay beside her. "They're alive?"

"Yeah, but we have them sedated. Seems they've got like a hive mind thing happening. They communicate through the implants in their brains."

Michael stared. "Really? Then there may yet be hope for the others."

David shrugged and led them to where Franklin lay, Erin monitoring him. "He's still unconscious. I've got the hypo but my scanners don't show what he was hit with, Michael."

He started the process of examining his patient then once satisfied there were no serious issues he accepted the hypo, removed the spent container and placed it into a hand-held medi-scanner. "A basic sedative. He'll be fine just a little groggy when he wakes."

"And the gun shot?"

"It was clean. In and out. He lost some blood, but that will heal. I've already applied antibiotics, I just can't dispense a painkiller, in case there's some kind of reaction."

"You're sure? No damage or long-term issues? Surgery?"

Michael shook his head, a small smile on his face. "He'll be sore and have a scar to talk about, but no, he'll be fine."

"Okay." The sour bile in her throat, the one she'd contained, reared up, and she pulled away, found a bush, and retched behind it.

A soft hand touched her shoulder. "Are you okay, Senna?"

The tears she'd held back spilled as Erin wrapped her arms around her and she gave in, whole body shaking as she cried.

"I didn't know what it was, and I held it in, Erin. I did my job, but I've never felt such *fear*. All because I love him and when Jonah said he was down..." Even now, the clutch of terror froze the marrow in her bones. She shivered while swiping at the tears that still dribbled down her cheeks.

"I know, Senna. I know."

Michael wandered over, his gaze traveling her face. "Better now?"

She nodded, feeling idiotic but also extremely grateful. "I need to inspect the site of the remains."

Erin's deep sigh had Senna turning. "They're pretty bad."

"I'm sure they are, but that's why I'm here, Erin."

Michael reached over with the bag and she accepted it, hand digging deep to pull out a bio-hazard suit, gloves and mask. The small scanner unit and batch of numbered vials.

"Is there someone who could assist?"

Michael grimaced. "I'll help you. Tell me what you need."

And she did. They set about retrieving the remains, piling them and laying numbers over them, she took bone samples once assured there was no easy way to take their identification and when the task was complete, he assisted in shrouding the pitiful bundles.

"No one deserves to end their lives like this," she spoke slowly as she discarded the protective wear in a pouch.

"No. But Erin just tagged me and Franklin's waking up."

Much as she wanted to be there for that, she bit her lip. "He doesn't know I'm here, Michael. I—and Jonah—decided my presence should be... covert, if you will."

He stared then laughed. "He's going to have his hands full with you, Senna." Then he enfolded her in a bear hug. "He'll be too grateful to see you initially. Once your back home though, you should tell him all."

"Yeah, everything." It was a promise.

They hurried back to the building and she stared at the remains, charred and still smoking before crouching down beside Franklin.

His eyes fluttered, and she couldn't help losing herself in them. The deep brown reminiscent of quality chocolate—a hidden weakness of hers. "Senna, what are you..."

"Shh." She laid her lips against his. "Later. Right now, I'm just pleased you're okay."

"I don't know what happened." He stared beyond her shoulder. "Michael?"

The big man knelt beside her. "You were hit with a hypo. Nothing serious but they had to get you out as the building caught fire."

"What about—"

"Later," Michael instructed. "I'm going to check you out again, then you're being airlifted back to base. Jonah's orders."

CHAPTER 21

The de-brief was an anticlimax as they gathered around. This time it was Senna's turn to care for Franklin. He'd shown a few low-level reactions to the anesthetic they'd hit him with, but Michael assured her they'd wear off soon.

Once back at the base and in a proper treatment room, Michael had given them some privacy. She settled beside his bed, the chair uncomfortable, and for the first time, she appreciated what he'd gone through when she'd been injured.

"Franklin, I have to tell you something." Her nerves jittered and jumped as he waited.

"Tell me anything, Senna."

She inhaled. "I was on the field. Jonah needed me... No, that's not quite true. I told Jonah he needed to know who was dead up there. He didn't want me to fight but..." She shrugged, not yet looking at him in case she lost her nerve now. "Anyway, we agreed I'd be waiting in the field where we were drawing out the children."

Franklin moved to lift up, and she stared at him, laying her hand against his chest.

"Stay. Let me tell you the rest first." She gulped. "I was supposed to remain in a non-combat role. I was going to babysit the historian, but things didn't quite go to plan. They started using incendiary devices, so I got him out and we ran. We made it up onto a ledge, and I hid him when I realized our people needed me."

He remained quiet, and she chewed on her lip. "Jonah and I kept it from you. We didn't want to worry you." Now she realized just how lame that sounded. "Then Jonah called, told me you were injured, and I was choppered in with Michael."

"Bare bones, huh?"

She glanced at his eyes, noting that they didn't glint with anger, and she let go of the fear that iced her veins. "You're not angry?"

"Oh, I'm furious. Don't get me wrong. You were injured, and you hid what you planned to do. I'd tan your hide if I could, but they've got me trussed up like a turkey." He sounded so thoroughly put out that she laughed and slid her fingers into his hand.

"I know what that feels like." The mirth died away, and she leaned down so her forehead rested against his. "I was terrified when he told me you were hurt and unconscious. I'm not sure how I'll cope in the future if you keep taking chances." They stayed like that for some time until Michael entered the room.

"Upsetting my patient, are you, Senna?"

She raised her head. "No. But I don't suppose you could spring him for the briefing?"

Michael smiled. "I was actually planning on just that. Come on, up you get, Franklin. There's not much more I can do, so head on over."

He pushed off the bed, dragged her close, and they made their way to the large tent where the briefing would take place.

This time, the media and key personnel were present, and the small room on the base couldn't contain those who needed to attend.

They slid into seating at the back of the area, the need to be there while Jonah presented what they knew was the death knell of the regime to the public.

It wouldn't be over fully until they'd rounded up all the combatants, but the air shivered with the anticipation and knowledge that the regime could no longer survive.

Jonah and Daniella had decided to hold the debrief and media conference out on the parade grounds so those involved in the actions could also attend.

Jonah fronted the podium, formally dressed and flanked by his wife Daniella in full senatorial mode. "Thank you all for your service. Today, we finally caught and subdued those behind the warrior children. We also made important strides in seeking to repatriate them into society."

At that statement, the media went wild, a frenzy of questions thrown at Jonah, which he ignored, waving his hands and waiting until they subsided.

"Yes, all the information will be released in due time. For now, be aware we have many combatants currently in secure facilities. We will be looking at their health and well-being. It may be that at some point we will consider fostering to carefully vetted families. More details on that will be forthcoming. However, for now, they are in a safe and secure environment. I can assure the public that at no point will we be using them as laboratory experiments. Each of these children deserve the chance for a future. To grow and mature and make their own decisions, free of coercion or threat."

Daniella stepped up, and Jonah moved along, to stand beside his wife. "The government of our world will be reinstated with all due speed. I will not be standing for election of president. Instead, I will seek to take on the role of senator with emphasis on the needs of the children and those displaced and affected by the war that has torn our world apart. I feel it is my part to help the healing process. I will, therefore, be removing myself from the Colony Ship committee. Our world now has the chance to grow, and with the opportunities offered to us with the colonization of other planets, our legacy must be that of peace. To that end, I feel the next colony ship should be named *Operation Homewoods* in honor of those who returned to service to assist in fighting for our freedom. They had already played their part, yet when the call went out, those who had done their part returned again to give yet more. I will be making representations concerning that once the first sitting of the government takes place. Now, it's time to look to the future."

A rousing applause washed over them as Daniella moved back to her seat. Jonah quieted the crowd. "I will also step aside once a replacement is sought. It was never my intention to lead the fight. I was not groomed for leadership and didn't seek it, and there are others far better qualified than I to take that mantle. However, I will remain until a suitable replacement can be named. As for Vandra Montaine, she is to be tried by a jury of twelve eminent scholars and justices. She will answer for her crimes against our world. As will Dr. Jeremy Colvert and those who've undertaken crimes of assorted abuses, murder, and code five breaches of the therapeutic policies."

The briefing went on for what seemed like hours, and Franklin held Senna's hand.

Once done, and the media dispersed, Jonah beckoned them. "Tonight we celebrate. We've achieved something momentous, and to be honest, I'd rather be among friends to share the moment with."

Senna grinned. "I thought you enjoyed the briefings. At the end there it felt like we attended one every day."

Jonah scowled. "I hated them with a passion, but with the way the ground rules kept shifting, they were a necessary evil. I'll be pleased to put this all aside. I have other plans for the future. Plans with my wife."

Franklin shuffled and Senna turned, concern battering at her. "What's up? Another reaction?"

He'd paled, and she reached with her hand to check his temperature. Her mind demanded she deal with this, when he shook his head. She frowned as the others around them suddenly appeared busy with something else. Her stomach curdled. *What could be going on?*

Franklin dropped to one knee, there on the ground, and her mind blanked, unable to believe what was happening.

"Wha—"

"Senna, I'm no prize. I'm not a senior officer or highly skilled. I'm not even sure what the future holds for me, but the one thing I do know is I love you. With my whole heart. I'd lay it at your feet or jump in front of a bullet for you."

"Franklin..."

"Let me finish, Senna." He spoke with an earnestness that tugged at her heart. "I can't imagine a world without you in it, and when you were lost, injured, my world ceased to exist. You're beautiful and wise, spirited and caring. Everything I never expected to find. Marry me?"

Blank. Her mind came to a complete stop. No thought whirred except here was Franklin, offering her the world. Himself. Everything she ever wanted from a life partner, and her brain refused to work.

"Senna?" He paled, half-rose. "An answer?" His croak betrayed his uncertainty.

Yes!

He blinked, gaze locked on her.

Realizing she'd screamed the word in her mind but hadn't yet answered, she opened her mouth, found it dry, and tried to swallow. She coughed, and someone shoved a tube of water into her hand.

Senna gulped gratefully, felt the moisture seeping into the membranes.

"Senna?" He started backing away, and she reached out and gripped his wrist, holding him still so she could finally answer.

"You don't get away that easily. I have yet to answer."

But he'd turned a sickly green, and she took pity on him as she smiled.

"Yes, Franklin."

His gaze narrowed. "Yes?"

She nodded. "Yes. I can't think of anything better than spending my life with you."

"You mean it?"

She sighed, cursing her inability to answer immediately. "Yeah, I do. So, you know, maybe we could go somewhere private and celebrate?"

Daniella cleared her throat. "Actually, I have a better idea. I mean, unless you want the whole nine yards, white gown, flowers, cake..."

Senna and Franklin turned. "What do you mean?"

"Well, the pastor who officiated for Erin and David is still here.

He couldn't get out. We've got a dress, if you don't mind borrowing, and we could—"

"Just a minute, Daniella." She turned to Franklin. "What do you think? After all, your uniform is here, right? There's a dress. We've got tonight and…" She whirled back. "Is the cabin still empty?"

Erin nodded. "Yeah. Likely to be for some time, so we could probably arrange for you to be billeted there. Both of you—as a married couple you're eligible for the building."

Excitement sparked through her veins like the bubbles in a fine champagne. "Franklin?"

"Let's do it."

So they did.

Did you enjoy this book by Imogene Nix?
There's more on the following pages. Just keep turning to see what else.

THE CELTIC CUPID TRILOGY

When Cupid—otherwise known as Diocail— is banished from his home on a remote Scottish Island, he's set a series of tasks by the great god Lugh, who also happens to be his father.

In *Blame The Wine*, he must bring two lovers together... BBW Cara and James, the man she's lusted over from afar who happens to be a super geek and head Veha Industries.

In *A Stranger's Embrace*, Diocail is driven to help an emotionally fragile Jane and Davis, a famous author. The task is more complicated, with the existence of Carstairs her could-be ex-husband and teenage daughter, Frannie.

In **Revenge on Cupid**, Diocail must take the ultimate chance and find his own happily ever after with Simone. Sometimes the past gets in the way and HEA's don't come cheap though.

The dusty, dingy little diner was full, even with its current state of cleanliness—or lack thereof. People from the surrounding offices didn't care about anything except the incredible, well-prepared food at a reasonable cost. They flooded in, like waves to the shore. As one tide left, another swept in.

"Honestly, Simone. I'm going to try getting his attention one more time. If that doesn't work, I'm out of there. I mean, how long can I keep trying?" Cara picked at the caramel tart she hadn't been able to resist with the cheap metal fork and flicked the blob of fresh cream that sat on top to the side of the plate.

"You've said that tons of times before. Besides, what are you going to do to get his attention? Hmm? Walk naked through the typing pool?" Simone bobbed the straw in her smoothie as she eyed her friend with a frown. "It's been what? Eighteen months since you saw him, and you've mooned over him from a distance ever since you met him. You need to move on, Cara. That is, unless there's something you haven't shared?"

The query was arch. Cara shivered even as she shook her head. "No."

Simone quirked an eyebrow, obviously unconvinced with the answer. Cara let out a deep sigh of frustration. "There's a position...it's only temporary, for a PA reporting directly to him." She speared a forkful of tart, chewed quickly and swallowed, before continuing. "In his office, full-time for the period of the engagement. I saw the memo yesterday. I mean, I have the skills, right? I can type, answer phones, make coffee, file, greet people. What's more, I can probably do it better than all those size eights in the typing pool that Ms. Jackman seems to prefer." She nodded thoughtfully. "All I have to do is get past the ogre in Human Resources."

Simone stared at her, disbelief clear on her face. "Girl, I so remember that woman. If you think you can get past her, you're doing better than I ever did. That's why I left Veha Industries, remember? Maybe it's time to haul out your resumé and consider some other options. Look for something better." Simone shook her head and billows of her crimson hair swirled through the still air.

Cara understood Simone only had her best interests at heart. But this time she knew the outcome would be different. Hell, she could feel it in the air. The tingle of expectation.

"Cara, the HR ogre will hang you out for breakfast before she offers you anything like a position in that office. Remember her mantra? Good looks and good work make for a positive workplace!"

Simone didn't sugar-coat anything. It was another great reason for their long- term friendship. Honesty. But Cara didn't want to hear the truth in the statement. Even if it was exactly as her friend said.

Cara nodded quickly. "Yeah, I know, but if I don't try, then I won't know how close I can get to him, right? And the only way to catch his attention is to get past *her* and see him in person." Cara quaked a little at the information she needed to share. The favor she needed to ask. "Anyway, I tidied up my resumé and dropped the application into a memo envelope yesterday, so it's too late to back out now. I mean, fortune favors the brave. Doesn't it? If I don't snag an interview, I'm going to visit the career advisor across the street and register with them." She shrugged. "I'll look for temp work until something more long-term shows up. I can see what they have on offer and well...who knows? Maybe a job with the right boss is just waiting for me. But I'd rather this worked out, to be honest." Her voice trailed off into a whisper. "I really wish he would notice me."

Simone took a long slurp of her banana drink, and Cara noticed her questioning gaze even as she squirmed. Finally, Simone nodded. "It's your funeral. So anyway, you'd better show me this memo if you want me to be a referee for you. I'm guessing that's what you need, right? I'll have to know what I'm supposed to say about you before they ring."

Cara smiled. "Thanks, Simone. I knew I could count on you." She slipped a piece of paper out of her handbag and handed it over. "Sorry it's a bit creased. It was in the bottom of my bag, I stashed it so none of the others from the pool would see. You know how it is."

Available from Love Books Publishing
books2read.com/CelticCupid

Direct Autographed Copy
https://www.imogenenix.net/CelticCupid

STAR OF ISHTAR

Warriors of the Elector
Book One

The first time Elara laid eyes on Grayson was when he rescued her from the clutches of a madman and his scientists who were kidnapping humans and conducting horrific experiments on them. That was years ago. In spite of her attempts to deepen their relationship, they remained nothing more than close friends.Now Elara is a medic with the Admiralty, and she knows what she wants. It's been Grayson since the beginning. When Elara is stationed on the *Star of Ishtar*, she arrives with a plan to further her career. But this time her plan has an added bonus—to finally get her man.

Grayson's spent years fighting the connection between himself and Elara. He's certain it only exist because he saved her life. But his will is failing, and he fears he just might give in to temptation.

"I finally made it." Elara Sudonne watched as the hull of the *Star of Ishtar* loomed in the inky darkness. She clutched her hands tightly together as the shuttle approached the hulking battleship.

This would be her new home and first combat ST placement for the Earth Empire. She quaked inwardly with nerves but fought to keep her serene exterior. Previously her deployments had consisted solely of on-planet expeditions and in rehabilitation and dirtside facilities. When the chance had arisen to move to the battleship, she'd grabbed it with both hands.

The frigid air chilled her bones as she sat in her shuttle seat, but a trickle of sweat inched its way down her back under the fresh gray wool flight uniform. Little puffs of vapor escaped her mouth as she rubbed her arms. Nerves stretched tight, she looked through the small portal at the front of the vessel. She wanted to tug at the collar that somehow seemed to have grown tighter as the ship loomed ahead, but instead she firmed her mouth, straightened her spine, and concentrated on the future.

"So damned long." She'd been working toward this outcome since the day Grayson Myatt and Duvall McCord had saved her from her Ru'Edan captors. She was lucky, she'd survived the 'experimentation' of the Ru'Edan leader Crick Sur Banden's scientists. "And all I have to remind me are my scars." She didn't grin at her own joke.

The person seated behind her jostled but she ignored it, lost in her memories. On that day, so very long ago, the young Elara, fresh-faced and with idealistic views of the empire, was taken from the mall where she'd been shopping with friends, thrust into the back of a transport vehicle, and given to the Ru'Edan scientists to experiment on.

For days they'd worked on her and others, seeking an average pain threshold of humans, slicing her skin then noting reactions and how long it took to heal. They'd cut her arms, body, and even her face, and now she carried the extensive scarring of the exercise as a reminder to herself and others of what they were fighting for. Freedom. The freedom of Earth and its allied planets.

She'd never relinquished hope, it had been her constant companion as she fought against the all-consuming terror. Then they'd found her in that dirty, disused warehouse. They'd found others too, in various states of death and decay. The smells of despair had filled the air with a fetid ripeness that she'd never been able to forget.

Since that day she'd promised herself that she would pay the Ru'Edan back for what they'd done to her. What they'd taken from her. Over the years, she tempered and honed the rage while remaining adamant that she would see the final act played out. She couldn't physically fight, but she had learned about trauma, knew it and understood how it affected a person, and used it as a weapon.

The iron will forged through her experiences had fed her determination, and she'd applied herself to study, finishing in the top ten percent of her class. She entered the medical program at the academy, working hard to excel. Her family remained supportive if perplexed as to why she had chosen to keep reminding herself of what had happened.

The maw of the *Star of Ishtar* loomed closer, opening its cavernous mouth as she watched through the portal. She could hear the voices of the shuttle crew signaling their intention to enter and land, the tinny confirmation coming swiftly. She watched avidly while the shuttle maneuvered, imagining the invisible shields dropping to allow it entry.

Her hands twisted with fear and anger, but she tamped down her emotions. Anger never helped anyone. Staying strong, knowing your history, and ensuring it couldn't be repeated, they were the answers, she told herself firmly, pulling herself from the grip of a dark past so horrific she still saw it in her dreams. She pushed it away to the recesses of her mind and focused on what she was about to do.

A squark overhead, the usual mechanical sound that alerted all on board to a transmission by the captain, caught her attention. "Attention all passengers. We are entering the shuttle bay. Please ensure when you disembark you remove all personal items. Move beyond the white line and wait for your designation."

The lights of the bay flashed as they entered, and once again Elara marveled at how far humanity had moved since they had first walked the Earth. She saw the opening of the structure as the shuttle moved into the bay, inching forward slowly until it stopped its ponderous motion and began its descent to the floor. Something deep inside warmed even as the shuttle's environmental systems began to synchronize with the cooler temperature of the *Star of Ishtar*, and she felt a smile crawl its way over her face.

Elara breathed in deeply, inhaling the metallic-tasting, recycled air and welcoming the calmness that settled on her body. Her eyes closed as she filled her lungs. "I'm here." There was more than a little satisfaction in her tone, and she smiled. She slowly exhaled, finding that center of peace she relied on.

A loud thud and clank echoed as the deep drone split the air. The engines were powering down, and there she was, on one of the Earth Empire's Emeritus class battleships. She sat in her seat, waiting for the all clear from the captain, and once it sounded through the cabin, she rose, tugging at the webbing belt and disengaging it.

The small backpack beside her was all she carried as she made her way to the exit, not needing to duck as so many others did. She stepped through the door, her hands gripping the rail of the cold, metal stairs which connected to the side of the gray shuttle.

She clambered down them slowly, savoring the experience. The sting of the cold on her hands from the stairs, frigid from even their brief exposure to the blackness of space, made her flinch inwardly. The shuttle journey from the Admiralty's strategic base at Aenna to their current position had taken just over an hour, but the whole time it felt like her heart had been in her throat. Her mouth was dry as she followed the new recruits from the ship into the landing bay. She stopped, silently noting the slight mustiness of the air, the recycled quality easily recognizable. Everything, including the oxygen, needed recycling in space.

All around her people swarmed, either around the ships or into the dogleg line that now formed ahead of her. Someone had opened the baggage locker of the shuttle, and the sound of dropping bags hitting the plascrete floor echoed in the air. Another crewmember guided trolleys to the other side of the shuttle, pulling out boxes with important day-to-day items for the ship, including vaccines and plants. She watched briefly, all the while listening to the alien cacophony. Voices called in welcome to old crewmembers, while new ones watched, many goggle-eyed in the fresh uniforms of newly minted officers and crewmembers.

Her gaze flicked around quickly, taking in the sights, sounds, and smells, pungent with oils and grease; burning smells from the scorched plascrete and the press of sweaty or nervous bodies. She joined the line silently, tacking onto the end, and stayed at parade rest, knowing the welcoming voice would cut through the air soon enough. She felt somehow disconnected from the main throng. Perhaps the knowledge that this was the outcome she had worked for years to achieve set her apart. However, still, she felt so...distant from everything around her. She smiled secretly at the bout of whimsy.

"Attention!" The voice boomed out over the plascrete of the docking bay, and she snapped her body into position, noting the commander who had bellowed the words. Technically, she outranked most members aboard the *Star of Ishtar*, except for the command and leadership staff, but she knew all newcomers had to join the welcoming parade, regardless of rank.

Fleet Captain Elphin came into view, his tired features topped by salt-and-pepper gray hair, which highlighted his cool blue eyes. Elara also recognized a body prone to a little middle-aged thickness. Following behind him was his second-in-command, Duvall McCord. A young up-and-coming officer, his status as a fast-tracking officer heading toward his own command, with Elphin both his mentor and captain, had become almost legendary at the academy.

She looked closely at McCord, noting the dynamic drive of his actions and movements. Soon he would achieve a promotion to captain, and she rejoiced for her friend. She'd followed his career with interest and had to tamp down a smile as his eyes betrayed the shock of seeing her before settling into their flat command persona. So he hadn't been apprised of her deployment, she noted, and she had to restrain the tiny feeling of surprise and satisfaction. She filed that snippet of information away.

She caught sight of the man standing behind Duvall. Grayson Myatt. He'd made her heart beat faster for years. Tall and blond with a muscular build and a sexy, tight, little butt, he had pools of deep-blue eyes that had always made her think of forever. He had a growth of stubble on his chiseled jaw, and her fingers itched to touch his perfect lips. Yes, since the day he'd found her in that nasty warehouse tied down like a ragged animal, she'd worshipped him from afar.

Now she had her opportunity to tangle with him, hopefully much closer than any chance that had ever come her way before. With a sigh, she pulled her gaze back to the captain and forced herself to concentrate on his words. She couldn't afford to have her commanding officer angry due to her being distracted.

"Welcome to the *Star of Ishtar*. Most academy recruits want to join us because of what we represent, but on this ship, we only take the best of the best. So, if you made it here, you're the ones we wanted to take a look at. Getting here is only the first step. Staying here is harder to achieve. Our people are the best. Earn your place, and in return, we'll make you one of our crew—a member of the *Star of Ishtar*. Only the best and the brightest wear our uniform and badge. You'll be expected to perform to your absolute limit then give some more. We don't tolerate people who don't pull their weight. Do us proud and wear your uniform with pride." The captain looked out over the new members of his crew. His voice had echoed during his speech, and now it died away.

He scanned the faces before him, and she could almost read his thoughts. There were new security officers and a smattering of other crew. Some of them were young and impressionable, and she knew a few wouldn't make the cut as crewmembers. Others would carve out their place on the *Star of Ishtar* and move to better positions and placements, like she would: the new SurgiTech, a younger female, experienced but untried on board a ship. She smiled at that thought.

Some of those who stood with her would be replaced as they failed the exacting standards the captain set. She'd heard that he was a firm captain, fair but demanding. He'd have to be to command this ship. The Ishtar had well over five hundred at full capacity, and the captain could select their placements as his command staff saw fit from the many who applied to join the crew. She sensed his satisfaction with the choices in the relaxation of his body.

Abruptly, he turned to Duvall, breaking her study of him. "Get them to where they need to present themselves." His words echoed as he walked away. He had a purposeful stride. Quick but unhurried, like he knew where he was going and how to get there. A man who knew how to get what he wanted. Someone to respect and admire.

"My name is Commander Duvall McCord. I am your second-in-command, and my direct subordinate is Commander Grayson Myatt. While you are aboard the *Star of Ishtar* you will be required to fulfill your duties efficiently. As Captain Elphin said, do your job right and you will be one of ours, with all the benefits that come with being a crewmember of the *Star of Ishtar*."

He paused and eyeballed each of the newer recruits, those fresh from the academy. Many of them paled under his gaze, and she smiled inwardly. Even the older people in the line seemed to quake beneath his scowl. He'd always had that air of innate authority, even when barely out of the academy himself. She knew his methods and watched him make full use of the carefully practiced tone of presence.

"Each of you has been assigned. You will present yourselves to the chief of your section. Those details will be found in your orders. Commander Myatt has organized a team to escort you to your cabins. You will have approximately one hour to prepare. We've arranged for crewmembers to escort you to your superiors. Be ready to present for duty. Any issues, you will, of course, take up with your section commander. Should there be need to take any further action, you will see Commander Myatt. You should only see me if you are a command crewmember or as a point of discipline. I am not one for small talk, so if you present to me, have a very good reason."

He delivered the words slowly and deliberately, and Elara restrained a small smile on hearing at least one gulp from those in the line nearest her.

"We run a tight ship here. Discipline and commitment are the two key factors we look for beyond loyalty in our crew. You will from henceforth represent our ship everywhere, and we do not tolerate anything less than the best." He looked around once more, the stern demeanor he wore so well reinforcing the message. If she hadn't known him for so long, she too might have missed the hint of humor glinting in his eyes, the one many took for coldness.

Her legs ached, and she wanted to move and relieve the pressure on them, but she held herself still, waiting for the command to dismiss. She wouldn't let herself or him down now. Not after she'd worked so long to achieve this position.

As the new ST, she had no previous experience on ships. She had vast experience in the field, but Elara was aware that would count for little in the eyes of most of the crew. She didn't intend to signal a weakness to anyone and least of all on her first day aboard the *Star of Ishtar*. That thought held her still and controlled.

She had big shoes to fill after her predecessor, Jamieson, had retired, even though she knew she could fill the void he'd left behind. As a long-term member of the crew—over twenty years—his tenure on the *Star of Ishtar* had placed him aboard since its launch. Due to his experience in the heat of battle with the Ru'Edan he had made a name for himself as the coldest of cold in the hottest of situations.

She hoped to emulate that herself and carve out her own place aboard the Ishtar, as its crew lovingly knew her.

Duvall and Grayson knew how much she wanted to prove herself. They just wouldn't have expected it here, on the Ishtar.

She watched Duvall study her, then, quickly turning on his heel, call to those assembled, "Dismissed."

Once they started to move away, she softened her stance, preparing to turn when the call came.

"Sudonne! A moment if you please."

Elara turned to face Duvall. "Commander?"

"Welcome to the *Star of Ishtar*, Elara. While I am surprised you're the new ST, Grayson and I are pleased you could join us. But how did you manage to pull it off? Keeping it quiet that you were the new ST?" he asked, his voice deep enough to make most women shiver with anticipation.

She smiled, thinking it was a shame she didn't have any feelings for him except sisterly attachment, but then again, given his lack of deep commitment to women, maybe it wasn't such a shame after all.

She understood what drove him. He wanted his own ship and to captain his own future. They'd spent many nights over wine or ale discussing his beliefs that commitment grounded a person. Inwardly, she shrugged. He'd make those calls for himself, though she was sure that one day he would come across someone who would make him consider his choices a little more thoroughly.

"I'm pleased to be here, Duvall. Having an uncle who happens to be an admiral, he was able to let Captain Elphin know that I wanted to surprise you. It's a small world in the Admiralty. Elphin already knew of me, so he okayed my placement. Once the powers knew there was no impediments to me joining the crew, it was fairly simple from there." She felt a small smile creep onto her face, then let it drop away. "What do you think Grayson thinks?"

"Ah, still chasing him, are you?" He grinned, his eyes twinkling. "I think he'll be pleased you're finally old enough and you're here." He looked her straight in the eye. "But you may just need to remind him of that particular fact." He motioned for her to go before him, barking out a deep laugh. "Come on, I'll show you to your cabin."

Available from Love Books Publishing
Available in Ebook via Books2Read

Direct Autographed Copy
https://www.imogenenix.net/Warriors1

THE BLOOD BRIDE BY IMOGENE NIX

Hope just wants to be an ordinary nestling. She went to college and escaped, but now she's back and there's a secret everyone is keeping from her.

Xavier is the new master of the nest, ready to welcome home the daughter of the house who he has never met. He's unprepared for the woman who steals his breath and enchants him.

Now Hope and Xavier must fight for lives and those of the innocents. After all, it is only by overcoming the rogues that they will have a chance of a timeless future together. But will it be in time?

PROLOGUE

As silence descended on the house, the shadows grew—dark grays and blacks that bled into each other. First one figure then another broke away, making a run toward the house. Silent as the grave, they moved swiftly over dew-slicked grass. Then they stopped still. Waiting. Not a movement betrayed them until a signal propelled them back into action and they started crawling upwards. The walls damp coating no barrier to the intruders that ascended in the darkness.

The sound of each window breaking shattered the quiet—the figures were inside. Screams echoed through the night. Yet, in this area of large estates, heavy with noise-absorbing shrubbery, no one could hear those within. The blood-curdling screams went on and on before finally dying away.

Just one sound echoed through the night: The sobbing of a child.

The front door opened and figures trooped out—ghostly specters against an inky night sky, broken by a single outline. A child in white, carried at the center of the pack.

No sound broke the silence as they moved toward the trees surrounded the house.

Flames now licked at the manor: A deathly glow of oily smoke rising.

All that remained was a single person—wrapped in a cape of midnight blue beyond the house—watching them melt away.

Jemima moved toward the burning structure, breaking into a run as she breached the threshold. Vainly she attempted to enter, but the heat drove her back.

Now dashing tears from her face, she raced across the graveled driveway toward the gates, where the guardhouse was located. No sign of life existed within the building and some instinct of survival slowed her pace to a careful creep. Out of breath and heaving from exertion, she nervously checked within.

Small puffs of white vapor colored the glass. She darted from one window to another. Her cloak drawn tightly around her body, hoping it would camouflage her from sight.

Satisfied, Jemima entered through the heavy, wooden front door and moved toward the phone she spied on the floor. Her eyes darting here and there she dialed, listening to the rotary motor as it returned to the proper position. Time was short and if *they* came back, she needed to have shared the message.

The phone rang once. Twice. With a brrping sound it connected.

"Hello?" A male answered and she felt a warm flush of relief at the voice. A voice she knew well.

"The manor has been breached. The girl child taken." The words erupted and her hand trembled.

"On our way." The click of the receiver being replaced echoed loudly in the stillness of the room.

Copper. She smelled copper.

Her stomach soured, knowing it meant more deaths. Jemima looked around for the gun—a gun with deadly, holy water-infused copper bullets—she knew was hidden somewhere in the room. A gun she couldn't find. *No divine intervention exists here*, she thought.

Hopefully *they* didn't remain. Feeding. If they were still here, that's what they would be doing. She found a corner and scrunched down, hiding from sight.

Crouched low, she tried to stay as still as possible, listening for sounds of the vehicles she knew would be coming. She dug her fingers into the flesh of her arms; remaining aware enough to stop before drawing blood. That would surely bring them out. Jemima dragged the cloak around her to capture the warmth, yet there was little to be found.

The sounds of engines roused her from the corner of the room. Jemima inched toward the window, the lead of the old glass distorting her view, hearing raised voices she knew Mistress Cressida had arrived.

Jemima retreated. Remained hidden from the woman because if she knew, all may well be lost. From the shadowed room she listened to the conversation...

"It smells like Estersham." The Mistress' eyes closed. "If it is, we have a problem." She turned once more, her face set and eyes now glacial in intensity. "James?"

The man nodded as if he knew what was to come.

"If I take those steps, I cannot return. Another must stand in my place." Her voice hardened while her eyes glittered in the dim light, piercing in their intensity.

Then the Mistress' voice called out in the near silence. "You and yours have been my loyal servants for so many years. I took an oath to protect you long ago. I renewed it with marriage and births, over and over. Now, my home and yours have been breached and this child taken from us. The girl child, who will be the hope and salvation of our kind, was ripped from the bosom of our nest. I will repay your loyalty and I will get her back." The words of power rippled in the night and licked at Jemima's skin.

Available in Ebook
books2read.com/BloodBride-Nix

Direct Autographed Copy
https://www.imogenenix.net/BloodBride

ALSO BY IMOGENE NIX

<u>Warriors of the Elector</u>

- Star of Ishtar
- Starline
- Starfire
- Star of the Fleet
- Starburst
- The Star of Eternity

The Star of Ishtar & Starline - Print

Starfire & Star of the Fleet - Print

Starburst & The Star of Eternity - Print

<u>Blood Secrets</u>

- The Blood Bride
- The Illuminated Witch
- The Sorcerer's Touch

<u>House Secrets (The Blood Secrets Continuation)</u>

- As Dawn Breaks (Coming 2021)
- Immortal Consequences (Coming 2021)
- Unnamed Book III

<u>The Automaton Series</u>

- Haven House (Coming 2022)
- Nobel Crest (Coming 2022)

The Search Duology

- Miss Elspeth's Desire
- Miss Isabelle's Craving

Reunion Trilogy

- War's End
- The Assassin
- Executing Justice

The Reunion Trilogy in Paperback

Sex Love & Aliens

- Tangled Webs
- False Webs
- Covert Webs

21st Testing Protocol

- Cyborg: Redux
- Children Of A Greater Evil
- When Evil Came To Stay (Not Yet Released)
- Finis: The War To End All Wars (Not Yet Released)

Webs Series in Paperback (coming 2021)

Celtic Cupid Trilogy

- Blame The Wine
- A Stranger's Embrace
- Revenge On Cupid

The Celtic Cupid Trilogy in Paperback

Zombieology

- The Reset (2018 - Love At The End of The World)
- I Dream of Zombies
- The Six Million Dollar Zombie

Knights of Pleasure

- Silken Knights (Not Yet Released)

Single Titles

The Chocolate Affair (also in Print)

Falling In Love Again (Previously A Sapphire For Karina)

BioCybe (also in Print)

Hesparia's Tears (also in Print)

Tomorrow's Promise

A Bar In Paris (also in Print)

Inheritance Of The Blood (also in Print)

The Plan

Loving Memories (also in Print)

Hero of Heartbreak Hill (also in Print)

My One & Only

Curse Bound (coming 2021)

Raspberry Dreams (Not Yet Released)

Non Fiction

Self Publishing: Absolute Beginners Guide (With Suzi Love)

Written as Ciara Cave

25 Curated Ways To Get Rid Of Telemarketers

Book Signings for Absolute Beginners

ABOUT THE AUTHOR

Imogene is published in a range of romance genres including Paranormal, Science Fiction and Contemporary. She is mainly published in the UK and USA.

In 2010, Imogene Nix (the pen name not Imogene herself) was born. Imogene sat down and worked tirelessly for 3 months culminating in the book Starline, which became the first in a trilogy titled, "Warriors of the Elector." Since then she's had over 30 titles published and is now focusing on hybridising herself - with a mixture of traditionally published and self-published works.

In fact, she's taking control of many of her back catalogue books, which are slowly re-releasing as self-published titles.

Imogene is a member of a range of professional organisations world wide, and believes in the mantra of mentoring and paying it forward and is actively involved in mentorship (through NaNoWrimo and her vlog: In The Chair With Imogene Nix) and tutoring of new and upcoming authors.

In her spare time she loves to drink coffee, wine & eat chocolate and is parenting her spoiled dog and a ferocious cat along with her husband and 2 human daughters and looks forward to weekends away with her husband in their caravan "The Seven Year Hitch!" Do look forward to her caravan romance at some point!

To Contact Imogene

www.imogenenix.net
imogene@imogenenix.net

facebook.com/ImogeneNix
twitter.com/ImogeneNix
instagram.com/ImogeneNix
bookbub.com/authors/imogenenix